MW00944816

THE GHOST OF OLD CENTRAL SCHOOL

by Deb Mercier
and Ryan Jacobson

Minneapolis, Minnesota

DEDICATION

For Jay. —Deb
For Jonah and Lucas. —Ryan

ACKNOWLEDGMENTS

A special thanks to my friends Elizabeth Hurley and
Dana Kuznar for helping me begin this story more
than 10 years ago, and to Darcy Halverson for all
the wonderful feedback and suggestions. —Ryan

Edited by Emily Beaumont
Cover by Y. Shane Nitzsche

10 9 8 7 6 5 4 3 2 1

ISBN: 978-1-940647-75-3
ebook: 978-1-940647-76-0

THE GHOST OF OLD CENTRAL SCHOOL

TABLE OF CONTENTS

How to Use This Book 5

Deductive Reasoning 6

Wednesday, 4:04 P.M. 8

Wednesday, 7:12 P.M. 29

Thursday, 7:41 A.M. 50

Thursday, 1:36 P.M. 77

Thursday, 6:02 P.M. 121

Epilogue 140

The Science of Deduction 146

The Empty Cabin (Preview) 150

About the Authors 152

HOW TO USE THIS BOOK

As you read this book, you'll sometimes be asked to jump to a distant page. Please follow these instructions. Sometimes you'll be asked to choose between two or more options. Decide which you feel is best, and go to the corresponding page. (Be careful: Some options will lead to disaster.) Finally, if a page offers no instructions or choices, simply go to the next page.

Along the way, look for suspects (people who might have committed a crime) and clues. You'll know when you've found an important clue *because it will look like this.* And you'll know when you're on a page that eliminates a suspect because you will see a magnifying glass in the bottom corner, just like the one below.

There are five suspects to find. One of them is behind the evil scheme. So keep track of all the suspects and all the clues because you'll need them to solve this mystery! A good way to do that is by creating a grid (like the one shown on page 7) on a blank piece of paper.

List every suspect, and write down any clues about them. Then cross out their names when you find proof they didn't do it.

GO TO THE NEXT PAGE.

DEDUCTIVE REASONING

Have you heard of Sherlock Holmes? The famous character from books, television, and films is a detective who solves mysteries by using a method known as deductive reasoning.

We all use deductive reasoning. In fact, we use it quite often—and probably don't realize it. "Deductive reasoning" means that we can draw a conclusion based on two or more true statements. Maybe that sounds complicated, but it's not. Check out these examples:

Statement #1: It's dangerous for people who cannot swim to jump into the deep end of the pool.
Statement #2: Barb cannot swim.
Deductive reasoning: It would be dangerous for Barb to jump into the deep end of the pool.

Statement #1: Basketball players get better at their sport by practicing every day.
Statement #2: Larry practices basketball every day.
Deductive reasoning: Larry is getting better at basketball.

Just as Sherlock Holmes does in his stories, you can use deductive reasoning to solve this book's mystery. You might, for example, meet a suspect who has big feet. Then you might find a clue that proves the criminal has tiny feet. Through deductive reasoning, you know the big-footed suspect cannot be the criminal. So you can cross that suspect off your list.

We've already told you that this story's villain will be one of the five suspects. So when you've crossed five names off your list, deductive reasoning tells you that the sixth suspect must be the villain! That is how you'll solve *The Ghost of Old Central School*.

Suspect	Clues	Proof
Deb	• Lives in Minnesota • Enjoys hiking • Plays the flute	
Emily	• Has dark hair • Goes to concerts	
~~Ryan~~	• ~~Big and tall~~ • ~~Writes books~~ • ~~Builds with LEGO~~	Criminal is short
~~Shane~~	• ~~Is an artist~~ • ~~Is very tall~~ • ~~Loves comic books~~	Criminal is short

A sample suspect list

WEDNESDAY
4:04 P.M.

Your name on the door says it all: Blaze Bailey, Kid Detective. You've been solving mysteries long enough to know when someone needs your help—and when someone is desperate for it. The tall blonde girl who's standing before you now (an eighth grader, by the looks of it) is definitely desperate.

"Can I help you?" you ask coolly.

She shifts her weight from leg to leg. Her big, brown eyes lock upon her fidgety hands. "I— I— I need your help," she stammers. "And I need it fast."

You stand and step away from your desk.

The office at the back of your parents' garage is small, and on days like today, you wish it were air-conditioned; your T-shirt feels like it's glued to your skin. But at least the garage is a place to call your own. Having an office has done wonders for business.

"What kind of help?" you say. "Did someone steal your homework? Do you have a secret admirer?" They're your most common types of cases.

"Nothing like that," she says shyly. "Have you heard of Old Central School?"

You nod. "Sure, it's in the middle of town. It's the one that might be closing."

"Do you know why they're going to close it?"

You quietly grind your teeth. It bothers you when you don't know something, and you don't know this. "To be honest, I go to Brown," you confess. "So I'm not sure. I suppose there's not enough money to keep Old Central running." It's the most obvious reason.

"That's what everybody thinks. They're not telling people the real reason."

"Oh, yeah, what's that?" you ask.

"Do you believe in ghost stories?" she says, finding more confidence.

It's a strange question, and it catches you off guard. You snort. "No, do you?"

She ignores your question. "Old Central is closing because of the school's ghost."

You try not to laugh. "A ghost?"

"That's why I'm here," she says. "Well, actually, that's why my dad sent me."

"Your dad?" you ask. You don't often get hired by adults. In fact, you've never been hired by an adult.

"It's complicated," she says. "The school board meets tomorrow night, and they're gonna vote to shut down Old Central. Before they do, my dad wants you to prove that someone is sabotaging the school."

"They're meeting tomorrow night? You want me to solve this mystery in one day?"

"My dad does," she corrects. "He can get you into Old Central tonight. Plus, there's no school tomorrow, so you'll have all day to look for evidence."

"That sounds a lot like trespassing—or breaking and entering. It could land me in trouble."

"Not if my dad is the school's superintendent," says the girl. "He can give you permission to be there."

You always try to play it cool with potential clients, but you can't hide your surprise. "The superintendent wants to hire me? Why? And why isn't he here himself? Why did he send you?"

She shrugs. "Like I said, it's complicated."

"I need more of an explanation than that."

She sighs deeply. "My dad can't be involved—not officially. Getting private detectives wrapped up in this mess could damage his reputation and ruin his career."

Now it's your turn to sigh. "So I have his permission, but if I get caught . . ."

"Then you're on your own," she finishes.

You don't say a word. You stay quiet until the long, awkward silence becomes more than she can bear.

Finally, she asks, "What do you think? Will you take the case?"

Take the case.

GO TO PAGE 58.

Turn down the case

GO TO PAGE 43.

Suddenly, the idea you've been trying to grasp locks into place. You've been searching for a secret location, but the tool wouldn't be hidden. It's a life-saving device for moments like this. It would be tucked away in an obvious spot.

Like the ledge above the door.

You lumber forward, half hunched over, unable to straighten your arms, legs, or back. You reach the door and stretch with all of your might. Every muscle within your body feels like it's tearing, yet you extend even farther, your fingertips fumbling around the ledge.

Thunk!

Something falls to the floor: a tiny, L-shaped tool.

Once again, hope pulses through you. You pick up the piece and try to fit it into the door's hole, but your nearly frozen fingers refuse to cooperate. It's like trying to tie your shoes while wearing a pair of oven mitts.

You blow into your hands. You rub them together. You stick them up your shirt. Anything to warm them. You try the tool again. This time, it slides into place. You're saved. But even after you turn the tool and hear the latch click open, the door doesn't budge. Something is wrong.

"Blaze," a familiar, muffled voice calls.

You glance at the window. Irene looks back at you. Her eyes are as big as golf balls, her mouth wide open.

You don't have the strength to wonder what she's doing here. "O-o-o-pen the d-d-d-oor," you stammer through chattering teeth.

"I can't." Her voice is frantic. "It's padlocked shut!"

That's impossible. If someone had stuck around long enough to padlock the door, you would have seen them.

You turn your attention back to the safety release. If Irene won't help, you'll do it yourself.

"Blaze, that isn't going to work," Irene tells you. "But there's another way out."

It gets your attention.

"Look above you," she says.

You do, and for the first time, you notice the giant, round fan built into the ceiling.

"The ventilation system," notes Irene. "If you climb inside, it can lead you just about anywhere in the school."

You stare at it for a moment. "H-h-h-ow d-d-d-o I get u-u-p th-there?"

Before Irene can answer, the fan starts to hum.

"Use the shelves like a ladder," she says. "But you have to hurry. The fan will start running in a few seconds—and when it does, you'll be trapped for good."

A horrible idea occurs to you. What if Irene is the culprit? What if she's behind everything? What if she's trying to get rid of you?

She didn't show herself—didn't suggest this new escape route—until you found the tool for opening the door. Maybe you were already on the verge of escape, and she's trying to sidetrack you. Maybe this is Irene's Plan B for eliminating you. After all, if you don't time it just right, you'll get caught in the middle when that fan starts spinning.

Do you trust Irene? Or has this case been a set-up all along? It's time to find out. One choice will lead you closer to the truth. The other will end in disaster.

WHAT WILL YOU CHOOSE TO DO?

Ignore Irene.

GO TO PAGE 33.

Trust Irene.

GO TO PAGE 46.

Principal Haysen is as good a candidate as anyone. She didn't seem like a criminal when you met her—a little weird, maybe. But that's certainly not a crime. You lead Irene to the center of the school. Just like yesterday, the dimly lit building feels creepy, even with Irene beside you—or perhaps because of her.

Still, as you approach the trophy case, your mind wanders to a chilling story you once heard about a school in El Paso, Texas.

Even as the students were gathering for a picture of their entire class, some of them felt nervous and uneasy. They couldn't figure out why, since the photo shoot was pretty ordinary—or so it seemed.

When the photographs were printed, there was an extra student in the pictures, a girl whom none of them had ever seen before. This girl was definitely not one of their classmates—and she hadn't been present when the photographs were taken.

You shudder as you pass the trophy case and arrive outside the school office. You peek through a window and see that it's empty. On the far end of the office, the doorway into Principal Haysen's room is dark. Maybe you're in luck, and the principal left school for a while. At the very least, she isn't in her office.

You sneak into the main office and scurry to Principal Haysen's door. It's locked, a good indication that the principal has left the building. Now, the question is how will you get inside?

A skeleton key would do the trick, except it isn't that kind of lock. At the place where a keyhole would normally be, there's a pad of numbers. This door opens with a secret code, rather than any key.

"That's advanced security for a school that's about to close," you say.

Irene shrugs. "The lock is new. She had it installed less than three months ago."

You turn and look at Irene. "Really? That's bizarre. What's she hiding in there?"

Irene shrugs. "Can we get in without the code?"

You shake your head. "No, but I bet Principal Haysen isn't the only person who has it."

You step over to the office administrator's desk and start looking for a clue. You flip through stacks of paper and rummage through drawers of supplies.

"What are you looking for?" Irene asks. "How will you know the code when you see it?"

"It's probably just a few handwritten numbers on a scrap of paper," you say.

You lift up the computer keyboard and take a peek underneath it. That's where you find it, written on a sticky note.

You peel the note off the keyboard and hold it for Irene to see. "This is the secret code."

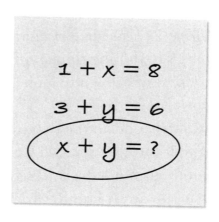

$$1 + x = 8$$
$$3 + y = 6$$
$$x + y = ?$$

"Do you know what it means?" asks Irene.

"I think so." You walk to the door and enter a code.

WHAT IS THE CODE?

7-3-1-0.

GO TO PAGE 40.

8-6-1-4.

GO TO PAGE 52.

You've encountered enough bullies to know how much trouble they can be, and you're sure some of them would love to prank their entire school. With that in mind, you decide to investigate Randall.

You hurry down the long corridor, toward the school's large trophy case at the center of the building. The lights are off; the hallway's only source of illumination comes from the evening sun shining through the windows. It leaves the corridor dim enough to look like the setting for a horror movie.

As you pass farther down the throat of the school, the thick, stuffy air turns musty. Old Central probably has air-conditioning, but it feels like they don't use it. The fact that you aren't familiar with the school's layout adds to your anxiety. You're relying on the details Irene gave you.

Near the center of the building, right next to the principal's office and a thick wooden door labeled "Custodians Only," you find what you're looking for: stairs. This is your route up to Randall's sixth-grade classroom on the second floor. You start upward.

Eeeeeee!

A terrible noise chills you despite the heavy air. From off in the distance comes the frantic sound of screaming.

Your instincts tell you to stay put, away from trouble. After all, screaming tends to attract adult attention—and the only adults in Old Central are the kind who would order you to leave. That would put an end to your investigation before it ever really began.

On the other hand, those screams might lead you to another clue. Or maybe someone's in trouble and needs your help.

WHAT WILL YOU CHOOSE TO DO?

Check out the screams.

GO TO PAGE 54.

Stay where you are.

GO TO PAGE 31.

"Ever since I started going to Old Central, I've heard ghost stories about it," Irene tells you. "The big rumor now is that it's haunted by a student from the 1990s."

You try not to roll your eyes as you wipe the sweat from your brow.

"She was all alone in the first-floor girls' bathroom," Irene continues. "She was looking at herself in the mirror, and her reflection somehow came to life. It reached out and grabbed her, and it pulled her entire body inside the mirror. She was never seen again, but her ghost is said to haunt Old Central. Pretty scary, huh?"

You chuckle. "Not really. Even if I did believe in ghosts, that story can't be true."

"Why not?" asks Irene.

"Because you said she was alone."

Irene tilts her head and squints. "So?"

"If that story really happened," you say, "and if the student was alone, how would anyone know about it?"

She stares at you blankly.

"You said she was pulled into the mirror," you note. "If no one else was with her, how would anyone know she got pulled into the mirror?"

At last, Irene smiles. "Oh, I see. How could there be a story if no one saw it and she never came back to tell it?"

You nod. "Exactly."

"But there's still a lot of other stuff," Irene insists.

"Like what?" you say.

"Strangely enough, it began inside that same girls' bathroom. Students complained about cold spots in front of the mirror. After that, things started to disappear. Kids lost pencils and notebooks, and teachers had their lesson plans taken. Chairs vanished, too."

"It could have been a thief," you say.

"Maybe, but the weird thing is a lot of the missing items showed up again a few days later—right before more stuff went missing."

"What else can you tell me?" you ask.

"Before and after school, we heard strange noises, like moans and chains and things."

"Where?"

"Everywhere. Then the lights started turning on and off, especially in the sixth-grade classrooms. And a creepy mist was seen floating through the gym."

Your head bobs as you say, "I've got it: cold spots, disappearing items, spooky noises, lights flickering, and a strange mist. Sounds pretty harmless. Anything else?"

"A bunch of students reported seeing a shadowy, dark figure roaming through the auditorium. It chased

21

them into the hallway and scared them so much that they refused to come back to school. The whole thing caused a panic. A lot of parents are moving their kids into different schools, and Old Central will be forced to close."

"So if I can prove these happenings are fake," you conclude, "the students come back to Old Central, it stays open . . . and your dad keeps his job."

"Right," Irene says.

"It looks like the next 24 hours are going to be busy. I need to pay Old Central a visit. But first, tell me about our number-one suspect."

"Who's that?" Irene asks, looking confused.

"The only person who can go anywhere in the school without creating suspicion: the principal."

GO TO THE NEXT PAGE.

You search the Internet for clues. You don't find much about any ghostly happenings.

You decide to take a different approach. You remind yourself that sometimes the best way to get information is to ask for it. The trick is finding the right way to pose your questions. No adult will help an unfamiliar kid investigate a ghost story. But most will jump at the chance to aid a child they believe has been wronged.

You run a few quick errands: You snap a photograph of Old Central. You buy a fancy picture frame, a red permanent marker, and a fourth-place ribbon. (First place is way too obvious.)

You eat dinner, and by 6 p.m. you're on your way to see the school's principal, *Ms. Haysen* (thanks to a home address Irene got from her dad).

Like any good kid detective, you've learned the value of fake crying. Adults will do just about anything for a crying child. You turn on the tears and step up to Principal Haysen's front door.

You give the door three sharp knocks.

A *thick, round, gray-haired woman* answers, wearing a purple velour sweatsuit. Blinking behind *enormous glasses*, she peers over your head, as if unfamiliar with the notion of having short visitors.

You clear your throat, and she focuses downward. "Yes?" she asks. She leans closer, studying your face. "Why are you crying? It's Wednesday. There's hardly ever anything to cry about on a Wednesday."

You're not quite sure what to say about that, so you stumble ahead with your plan. "I'm so sorry to bother you, ma'am, but I'm hoping maybe you can help me." You add a sniffle for effect.

"Come back on a Thursday. Maybe then I can," says Principal Haysen. She moves to close the door.

"Wait!"

She swings the door back open and stares at you, pushing her glasses up her nose. She sighs. "What is it that's so important?"

"It's just, well, um," you stammer, "this." You pull the picture frame out of your detective bag and hold it up for Principal Haysen to see.

She squints at the photo. "How unfortunate."

Unfortunate? That's it? It's not what you expected.

Inside the fancy picture frame is a snapshot of Old Central, the one you took less than an hour ago. You printed it from your computer, framed it, and slapped a fourth-place ribbon on its side. (The yellow ribbon gives the whole thing a "special" look—like it's an award-winning picture.) As a final touch, you scrawled the words "I HATE OLD CENTRAL" over the entire thing with the red marker.

Your idea was to make Principal Haysen believe that someone ruined your beautiful work of art. But apparently, she will only care on a Thursday. Now, it's time to salvage your plan.

You sniffle and exhale deeply. When you speak, your voice quivers. She's really going to make you work for this. "I'd like to know who did it," you say. "So—so I can tell my dad."

Principal Haysen hesitates. The door wavers in her hand, as if part of her wants to shut it and part of her wants to keep it open. "Who is your dad?" she asks. She leans in close and whispers, "Is he a Scorpio?"

You take a half-step back. *A what?* you think. You have no idea how to answer this. Talking to the principal makes you feel like you went down the rabbit hole with Alice. "Um, Mike Bailey. And . . . yes?"

Principal Haysen smiles widely. "Well, why didn't you say so? I'm always happy to help a fellow Scorpio."

She pats your back tenderly. It's like being comforted by a giant grape. "I'm very sorry about your lovely photograph. What's it for?"

Now you're getting somewhere.

"It's for my young photographers' group," you say. "We meet after school on Mondays. We had a contest, and I won fourth prize. My picture was hanging at the history center, but then this happened."

The principal shakes her head gravely. "Must have happened on a Tuesday," she mutters.

You plow ahead, fake crying a little harder. "Is there anyone who doesn't like your school? Maybe they did it." You hiccup.

She pauses for a moment, biting her bottom lip. "The school is closing. Who doesn't like Old Central? I have no idea who would do such a thing."

You turn the picture toward yourself and stare at it with your saddest eyes. You let your shoulders sag. "Thank you anyway, ma'am." You turn away slowly, dragging your feet. "My dad will be so disappointed."

"Unless . . ." Principal Haysen says.

Yes? you think.

"This stays between us," continues the principal. "And only because it's Wednesday." She beckons you closer. "There's a *sixth grader named Randall March*. He's kind of a bully," she whispers. "I don't think he likes Old Central. I don't think he likes much of anything."

She considers for a moment. "Except *he likes rabbits.*"

You nod, as if what she said makes perfect sense. At least you got a name. Maybe you can get another one.

You stammer, sounding heartbroken and desperate. "The picture was hanging pretty high on the wall, so this might have been done by a grown-up. Do you know any grown-ups who don't like the school?"

Principal Haysen rubs her chin. "Between us?"

"Of course."

The principal leans out her door; she looks first one way and then the other way down the street. "*Mr. Jenkins* is not happy," she says.

"Who is Mr. Jenkins?"

"You say your dad is a Scorpio?"

"Yes."

She nods. "Well, then, Mr. Jenkins is our *custodian*. Even before we decided to close the school, we were going to cut his job at the end of the year. When I told him, he gave off very bad vibes."

"Does Mr. Jenkins still work there?" you ask.

"Yes, until the school officially closes . . . or until Sagittarius rises."

Perfect. You have the information you came for (plus some serious strangeness). You thank the principal and excuse yourself as quickly as you can. When you're a block away from her house, you stop to add the names to your list of suspects.

So far, your investigation is off to a solid start.

GO TO THE NEXT PAGE.

WEDNESDAY
7:12 P.M.

The evening air is still sweltering. You creep through the parking lot outside the school, crouching low to the ground. You note three cars parked there. It means at least three adults are inside.

You jot down the license plate numbers. The pen ink smears under your sweaty hands. With the hot sun beating down and the steamy parking lot underfoot, you feel like you're in the middle of a grilled cheese sandwich. But this information is worth getting. You never know if you'll need it later.

Finished, you slide your notepad back into your bag, and you hurry to the school's nearest side entrance—the door that was left unlocked for you. As you step inside, you can't help but feel nervous. It's strange how large, old buildings always seem so eerie. You have to remind yourself that you do *not* believe in ghosts, and you continue forward.

Your plan is simple: Snoop around, stay away from anyone old enough to drive a car, and finish your secret investigation before tomorrow night's board meeting at 7 p.m. Piece of cake . . . right?

As you stare down the long hallway, you realize that you have a lot of work to do. Old Central is a very large school. It seems even bigger because all the classrooms are divided among three floors. That certainly won't make your search for clues any easier.

The good news is Principal Haysen gave you a couple ideas of where to begin. Thanks to her, you have two more suspects: Randall March and Mr. Jenkins. You can begin by looking for clues in Randall's sixth-grade classroom or in Mr. Jenkins' custodian closet.

WHAT WILL YOU CHOOSE TO DO?

Investigate Randall.
GO TO PAGE 18.

Investigate Mr. Jenkins.
GO TO PAGE 63.

You've always trusted your instincts. There isn't any reason to stop now. You stay where you are—it's best to wait until the commotion dies down before you do anything further.

After a few seconds, the screaming stops. You hear footsteps trample quickly through the hallway and out the main doors. It definitely sounds like someone got spooked by something.

That means the trouble probably isn't over. Whatever did the scaring is almost certainly still in the school. You wait a few minutes longer before continuing.

"You there," says a voice from behind. "What are you doing?"

A second too late, your brain tells you to run for it. But your instincts cause you to spin toward the voice.

"You?" says Principal Haysen. She's traded that purple sweatsuit for slacks and a flowery blouse. She peers at you through her thick glasses. "I remember you. Why are you here?"

It only takes you a moment to come up with a cover story. You put on an innocent smile. "Oh, hi, Principal Haysen. I wanted to get some photographs. You know, before the school closes. The natural lighting at this time of night is perfect. I hope that's okay."

She crosses her arms. "How did you get in here? The doors are supposed to be locked—especially on Wednesdays."

"I came by to take some more photos of the school, and I saw a few cars parked outside," you say. "So I tried one of the doors, and it was open."

Her confused expression clears, and she unfolds her arms. She believes you—or so it seems. Then she tilts her head, as if listening to a voice you can't hear.

"Where's your camera?" she asks.

The principal is smarter than you thought.

DO YOU HAVE A CAMERA?

Yes.

GO TO PAGE 44.

No.

GO TO PAGE 67.

You shake your head. "No, I don't believe you."

She begins to protest, but you ignore her. You twist and turn the L-shaped tool, but the door will not budge. You remove the tool and carefully place it again into the opening in the door.

Nothing seems to work.

You're no longer certain if Irene is still here. You can't see or hear her.

You try to focus, but your brain is too fuzzy to think. You're too cold, too uncomfortable. In fact, your body is so cold it burns. But that doesn't make sense, does it? You're not sure.

As your arms and legs grow numb, you slide gently to the floor. Everything begins to move in slow motion. All you can think about is how tired you are. Rest, you need to rest. You allow yourself to lie down. You put your head on the floor. It should feel cold, yet you feel nothing at all.

Your eyelids grow heavy, so you squeeze them closed. You find yourself drifting into a deep sleep, one that will never end.

GO TO PAGE 68.

For a moment, you consider running. You'd love to ask the student a few questions—to find out what he knows—but why? He obviously encountered something spooky. Whatever it was, it might still be in the gym. Maybe you'll see it for yourself. At the very least, you hope it left a clue.

GO TO THE NEXT PAGE.

You step through the gymnasium doors and scan the large room. Its vast emptiness is chilling. There is nothing here. And no one.

Except the door on the far wall—it's open.

As with so many other schools, Old Central's gym doubles as the cafeteria. (Irene told you as much.) The open door leads into the kitchen. It's probably where the "ghost" was hiding before it scared the student.

You step across the vacant space, once again wiping sweat from your brow. Your damp clothes are starting to stick again—you hate that feeling. But it's nothing compared to the clap of your feet against the white-tiled floor. The haunting echo causes goose bumps to form on your arms. You silently scold yourself for allowing Irene's ghost story to get to you. You try to shake off your fears. There's work to be done.

For 10 minutes, you study the kitchen. The setting makes you think of a ghost story you know, set in the town of Harrison, Michigan. *A woman, Mrs. Reinke, had just returned from a grocery store and was filling the cupboards with food. When she turned around, she spied two 6-year-old twins standing before her.*

The mysterious girls moved toward Mrs. Reinke, their hands clasped together as if playing a game of Red Rover.

Before the woman fully realized what was happening, the children were upon her—and then behind her. They had passed directly through her.

A terrible chill swept over Mrs. Reinke. She spun in time to see the girls disappear through the wall and into the backyard. Mrs. Reinke raced to the window, but the children had already vanished.

You shake such ghostly thoughts from your mind. Instead, you think of your mom and how proudly she brags about her "neat freakiness." Even she would marvel at how clean this kitchen is. There isn't a spoon out of place, let alone any evidence of a ghost. In fact, there's no evidence that anyone else was here. Ever.

The only place left to search is the walk-in freezer. It's like a super-cold refrigerator the size of your bedroom. You open the door, and a frigid breeze blasts you. It stings your nostrils and takes your breath away. You step inside. The sweat pouring from your body turns to ice. Your wet clothes become hard and crunchy. You are instantly uncomfortable. You wish you had a jacket. And mittens. And a stocking cap.

It's only a few seconds before your body begins to shiver. You'd better make this quick. You hurry across the room, scanning the shelves that line the walls, looking for anything out of the ordinary. Each of your breaths puffs into a tiny, visible cloud. Other than that, you see nothing more interesting than a stack of frozen pepperoni pizzas.

Your arms and legs stiffen. Your body slows down. "Time to get out of here," you tell yourself.

You turn back toward the freezer door—just in time to see it slam shut.

"No!" you shout. You step toward the entrance, but your muscles feel tight—you may as well be running in slow motion. You lunge into the door, shoulder first, praying it will open.

It doesn't. You're trapped, sealed inside an icy tomb.

You peek out the door's tiny, square window, hoping to see a cook who locked you in by mistake. No one is there. You are completely alone. As you crumple into a ball on the icy freezer floor, you become quite certain that you're going to die.

* * *

Hypothermia is a dangerous medical condition that occurs when victims' body temperatures drops below 95 degrees Fahrenheit. They shiver, become clumsy, and have trouble thinking. They grow tired, and soon their heart and lungs stop working. Eventually—if they don't warm up in time—they die.

Judging from your symptoms, you're experiencing the early stages of this condition. You consider digging into your detective bag, but you already know nothing in there can help. You're locked in a freezing cold vault, one that no wireless signal can penetrate. There's no way to call for help and no way to open that door. Or is there?

You study the entrance's flat, metallic surface. There's no handle to push and no knob to turn, but the news isn't all bad. You spy a tiny, octagonal hole in the place where a doorknob would typically be. You recognize the hole as a safety release, built just in case anyone ever got trapped in here. It means that, hidden somewhere in this freezer, there's a tool that fits perfectly into that hole, a tool that will unlatch the door and allow you to escape. You need to find it.

Your renewed hope warms you, if only for a moment. You begin ripping into the boxes of food, checking them inside and out. You scan every inch of shelf space. You search every corner of the room. You find nothing.

Where could they have hidden the tool? You try to guess, but every thought slips away like a fish through wet hands. The frigid air has begun affecting your brain, as well as your body.

You concentrate harder. You're missing something, and you know it. There has to be another hiding spot, something you overlooked.

An idea begins to form in your mind, but it's jumbled, scrambled. If you focus, maybe you can unscramble the message that your brain is trying to send.

O L O K   A V E B O   H E T   O R O D

CAN YOU READ THE MESSAGE?

Yes.

GO TO PAGE 12.

No.

GO TO PAGE 56.

You carefully type in the code: 7-3-1-0.

The keypad is illuminated by a blue interior light for a moment, and the door clicks open.

"You did it," Irene says gleefully.

You offer her a wide grin. Then you extend your arm forward and politely say, "After you."

The lights in Principal Haysen's room are off, but the morning sunlight shines in, allowing you to see.

"What are we looking for?" Irene asks.

You shrug. "We'll know it when we find it—I hope."

You scan the room. Nothing seems suspicious or out of place. There isn't even a big painting on the wall to hide a secret safe. It's just a standard, boring office. So what's with that high-tech lock on the door?

You march to the closet and swing open the door. You want to find a ghost costume hanging there, so you can call this case closed—but no such luck.

Next, you turn your attention to Principal Haysen's desk. It definitely feels weird to snoop around like this, especially if she has nothing to do with the school's ghostly problem. But you remind yourself that you have Superintendent Gorter's permission—and he's Principal Haysen's boss. That makes you feel better. Besides, this is just a job, nothing personal.

You scan the desktop, but there isn't much to see. It's almost as tidy as the kitchen. Principal Haysen is an organized person. Still, there must be something here. Why else would a person need a secret code to get inside?

You wiggle her computer mouse to wake up the system. Not surprisingly, the monitor comes alive to reveal a password screen. A person who utilizes a high-tech locking system is not someone with an obvious code like "password" or "1-2-3-4-5." It's worth try, but you're denied entry both times.

You glimpse the public address (or P.A.) system, which is used for making schoolwide announcements.

An idea forms in your mind. "Irene, did you say the spooky ghost noises seemed to come from everywhere?"

"Yes, they've been heard all over the school."

You point to the P.A. system. "Could they have come from here?"

She thinks for a moment, then nods. "That makes sense. If Principal Haysen—or someone—played ghost sounds into there, everyone in the school would hear it."

"Right," you agree. "And if the sounds were played when only a few kids were in the building, they wouldn't know it's being broadcast everywhere at once. They'd think they were hearing a ghost nearby."

"Now we know what we're looking for," says Irene, "something that plays scary noises."

You find a mobile phone in the first desk drawer you open. You activate its music app and scan through all the playlists. One of them is titled *Halloween Sound Effects*.

"This is it," you say, holding up the phone.

"I guess we know who's behind the fake haunting," she replies optimistically.

You shake your head. "Maybe, and maybe not. Sure, the principal could've had this phone for weeks. Or she could've taken the phone from someone yesterday. And you said the noises were heard before and after school, at times when Principal Haysen may not have been in her office. We snuck into here without much trouble, so someone else could do the same."

"I suppose you're right," says Irene.

"And one more thing," you add, "the phone has a name on it. It belongs to Randall March."

GO TO PAGE 66.

Your instincts tell you there's something fishy about this girl. She's not telling you the whole truth. Maybe she's lying altogether. Either way, the feeling in your gut says her case is bad news.

"I'm sorry," you reply. "This doesn't sound like something I can help you with."

You expect her to protest—to complain, to beg, to do anything. But she stands emotionless and unmoving. Now the awkward silence bothers you.

You turn around and walk to your file cabinet. You dig through the top drawer while you tell her, "I can recommend a few other detective agencies. I'm sure one of them would be happy to—"

Your sentence hangs unfinished. You spin back to where the girl once stood, but she is no longer there. She left without even saying goodbye. Not that you blame her. You shrug and return to your desk. There's work to be done.

As you sit, you can't help but wonder what would've happened if you had taken the case. It's an interesting question, but the answer is one you'll never know.

GO TO PAGE 68.

You reach into your backpack and pull out your nice camera. You hold it up and say, "Right here."

Principal Haysen smiles. "I should be upset, but everyone knows the approach of the waxing crescent moon is no time for negativity."

You're not sure how to reply, so you remain silent.

"I have a *passion for photography* myself, you know," continues the principal. She looks over your shoulder, down the hallway, seemingly in her own imaginary world. "And this old school really is quite beautiful. It's a shame that . . ."

She doesn't finish her thought. "Regardless of your reason, you shouldn't be here. I'll have to ask you to kindly leave in a non-negative manner."

"Oh, okay," you say, trying to sound both surprised and disappointed. It's not a stretch. "I'm supposed to go home before it gets dark outside anyway."

The principal smiles again. "Come back after school some time soon, and I'll give you a tour personally. If you listen closely, this building whispers its secrets, you know." She nods as if imparting important wisdom. "There are some very interesting nooks and crannies in this hallowed place."

"Sure. I'd like that very much," you say.

You worry that she may decide to escort you to the door, so you turn and walk away as quickly as you can—without moving so quickly that it seems suspicious.

Of course, you have no intention of leaving just yet. But you do need to stay away from Principal Haysen's office now, so you walk toward the area where the screaming came from: the gymnasium.

GO TO PAGE 35.

Irene's arrival has left you with plenty of questions, but you decide to trust her. You hope you don't come to regret it. You grab the emptiest set of shelving—it hurts to flex your fingers—and you drag it to the center of the room. Above you, the fan's hum grows steadily louder.

"Hurry," calls Irene. "You're running out of time."

You move forward, but the cold air has made you clumsy. You barrel into the shelves with too much force. You almost knock the entire thing over.

"Be careful," Irene says.

You turn back toward your makeshift ladder and, more cautiously this time, crawl upward. As quickly as you can, you reach the top and stretch your arms past the blades. You grab the ledge beyond it. That's when you catch the mechanism's first hint of movement. You instinctively pull back your hands—you don't want them to get cut (although your extremities are so numb that you probably wouldn't feel it).

Your quick movement knocks you off balance. You teeter toward the floor, catching yourself and stealing another glance at Irene.

"Go," she orders.

You take a deep breath, turn back toward the fan, and launch yourself. You reach inside once more, but this time you don't hesitate. You pull yourself through the opening, even as the blades begin to whirl.

For the briefest of moments, you imagine what would happen if they began spinning at full speed. You quickly climb, pulling your legs into the air duct just as the fan kicks into gear. You were milliseconds away from disaster, but you've made it.

Crawling through the tight, metal air duct system is miserable. More than once, you imagine yourself getting stuck. Fortunately, your time inside is short.

Within minutes, you find a way out: a vent that leads into a dark, empty room.

You're cold, you're tired, and your energy is sapped, but the vent's cover comes off with surprising ease. One kick and it crashes to the floor below. You climb out and carefully lower yourself.

A blur of motion catches your attention. Someone is standing in the darkness. You jump backward, preparing for a ghost . . . danger . . . you're not sure what.

You peer through the darkness and realize that you are not face-to-face with another person. Rather, you're looking at a mirror, at your own reflection.

You scan the rest of the room, noticing a row of sinks and a wall lined with six toilet stalls. You're in one of

Old Central's bathrooms—and judging by the lack of urinals, it must be the girls'.

Irene's ghost story flashes through your mind, and you take another step back. Alone and in the dark, it's almost too much to bear. You start toward the door, but then you remember the cold spots. You look up at the vent, nodding. You know where the cold comes from.

Right before a class takes its bathroom break, the "ghost" blasts the air-conditioning for a few minutes. Students step in from the hot, stuffy hallway and presto: instant cold spot.

You want to investigate the air-conditioning controls, but you're in no shape to continue. Besides, you have another clue to follow: the license plates. Obviously, the "ghost" is in the building, and when you find out whose cars are parked outside, you'll have more suspects.

And speaking of suspects, you'd like to ask Irene a few questions. Unfortunately, as you exit the restroom, she is nowhere in sight.

You sneak back to the kitchen. Irene isn't here either. You investigate the freezer door. The padlock is gone—assuming there ever was a padlock.

Feeling tired and vulnerable, you hurry out of the school. The night air welcomes you like a warm blanket.

$* * *$

Back at home, you grab a snack and then escape to your office. A quick phone call to your cousin (who happens to work at the county sheriff's office) reveals whose cars were parked at the school:

1.) Mr. Jenkins

2.) Principal Haysen

3.) *Ms. Sanderson, the media specialist*

That's another suspect for your list. And given that someone tried to turn you into an ice cube, you intend to investigate every clue to its fullest.

Your next decision is also an easy one. You add one more name to your list of suspects: *Irene Gorter.*

GO TO THE NEXT PAGE.

THURSDAY
7:41 A.M.

Before you slip back inside Old Central, you peek at the parking lot again. The same three cars are there. You zip through the doorway. The hall is dim and completely empty, except for one person: Irene.

She smiles and waves. "I was wondering when you'd come back."

"Why are you here?" you bark, not bothering to disguise your mood.

She takes a nervous step away from you. "Are you mad? I was expecting a thank you."

GO TO THE NEXT PAGE.

You want to ask her a hundred questions. But you might learn more by letting her tag along. Of course, that's the sort of plan that could get you hurt—or worse. Should you ask your questions, find out what you can, and be done with her? Or should you play along and see what you might learn?

Confront Irene.

GO TO PAGE 57.

Let Irene stay.

GO TO PAGE 65.

You carefully type in the code: 8-6-1-4.

The keypad is instantly illuminated by a red interior light, and it starts to beep.

"What happened?" asks Irene.

Each beep grows louder and louder.

"I must have typed it wrong," you tell her.

You try it again: 8-6-1-4.

The beeps are replaced by a loud, wailing siren. You plug your ears and shout, "That was the wrong code! Let's get out of here!"

As quickly as it began, the piercing noise stops. You pull your hands off your ears and look at Irene with confusion.

"You there," says a voice from behind. "What are you doing?"

A second too late, your brain tells you that you should run for it. But on instinct, you spin toward the sound of the voice.

"You?" says Principal Haysen. "I remember you." She puts her hands on her hips. "Step into my office. That's where you wanted to go, right?"

She grabs your arm and squeezes. You watch as she enters the code: 7-3-1-0. She doesn't let go of you until she's pulled you into her room and sat you in a chair.

Irene follows you both inside, looking dejected.

"Shall I call your parents, or shall I call the police? What's your name and your parents' phone number?"

You have no choice but to tell her. You will be in (slightly) less trouble if your parents come and get you here versus coming to get you at the police station.

Everything that follows feels like a bad dream. There is a long and awkward wait, the principal glaring at you with icy eyes. Then there are your parents, apologizing to Principal Haysen, raising their voices at you, and driving you home. There is your office in the garage getting taken apart, item by item. There is your "Kid Detective" sign being torn down for good.

Your mom and dad have put you out of business. Your investigation into the Ghost of Old Central School is at an end.

GO TO PAGE 68.

Screaming—that can't be good. It almost certainly means trouble, perhaps even danger. But it also probably means a clue. You can't risk missing it.

You rush toward the sound. The cry grows louder, and you push harder. You run as fast as your legs will take you. Sweat drips into your eyes, stinging you for a moment. You blink the pain away and keep moving.

As you draw closer to the gymnasium, you realize the scream is coming from within. The gym doors are dead ahead, just a few strides away. In five seconds, you'll be there.

Before you get any closer, the doors swing violently open, slamming against the wall. Frantic wails of terror fill the hallway, as a student bursts from within. You recognize him from an Internet search you did at home: It's Randall March. He's *tall for his age with an athletic build*. He wears an expression of shock and terror.

The dark-haired boy stampedes toward you, and you leap out of the way. He shouts, "Ghost! Run for it!" as he blows past you. Randall must have *twisted his ankle or hurt his foot. He's running with a limp*.

For a moment you're stuck in place—not from fear but from indecision. Should you chase Randall and find out what he knows, or should you enter the gymnasium and see for yourself? The first option might ruin the secrecy of your investigation. The second might put you in danger. Either one could end in disaster, but you are running out of time to make a decision.

WHAT WILL YOU CHOOSE TO DO?

Chase Randall.

GO TO PAGE 61.

Enter the gym.

GO TO PAGE 34.

You try to focus, but the idea eludes you. You are too cold, too uncomfortable. Your brain is too fuzzy to think. Your body is so frozen it burns. But that doesn't make sense, does it? You're no longer certain.

A thought slowly becomes clear in your brain. *Look above the door. Look above the door. Look above the door,* it echoes.

The idea comes too late. As your arms and legs grow numb, you slide gently to the floor. Everything begins to move in slow motion. Even the strange sound—is someone calling your name?—it seems to take several minutes to register in your mind.

All you can think about is how tired you are. Rest, you need to rest. You allow yourself to lie down. You put your head on the floor. It should feel cold, yet you feel nothing at all.

Your eyelids grow heavy, so you squeeze them closed. You find yourself drifting into a deep sleep, one that will never end.

GO TO PAGE 68.

You laugh, although you don't think the situation is very funny. "A thank you?" you snap. "You tried to kill me and you want a thank you?"

Irene gasps. "You think I tried to kill you? That's ridiculous."

"Is it?" you say. "I don't know if you're behind all of this. And, to be honest, I can't prove that you're the person who locked me in the freezer. But one thing is certain: I don't trust you. So why don't you stop wasting my time, and tell me what's really going on here?"

Her eyes begin to water. She takes a deep breath and swallows hard. She closes her eyes for a moment. When she opens them, she appears suddenly calm.

"I'm sorry you feel that way," she says evenly. "You aren't the person I thought you were. I won't waste any more of your time . . . because you're fired. I want you off this case. You no longer have permission to be here."

You begin to protest. You try to apologize to her, but it does no good. Irene simply turns and walks away. She ignores you, never looking back.

With one bad choice, your investigation is over. You'll never learn who was the Ghost of Old Central School.

GO TO PAGE 68.

You smile. "Yes, I'll take it."

"Thank you!" she exclaims. She starts forward as if to hug you. She stops, apparently changing her mind. Good thing—it's way too hot for hugging.

"What happens next?" she asks.

"For starters, you can tell me your name."

"Oh, sorry. I'm Irene Gorter."

"Nice to meet you, Irene. I'll need to pack supplies for the case. In the meantime, tell me everything you can about your school's ghost."

Irene nods eagerly, and as you begin to fill your detective bag, she shares quite a tale.

GO TO THE NEXT PAGE.

Use a blank sheet of paper to create a suspect grid, as shown on page 7. Then choose five items from the list below to carry with you during the investigation. Note these items on the back of your paper.

Camera: Being a detective isn't just about learning the truth. You'll have to prove it. A picture of the "ghost" might be the evidence you need.

Mobile phone (no camera): Reception is poor inside Old Central. But if you get into trouble and if you can get your mobile phone to work, it might save your life.

First aid kit: Serious cuts and bruises may keep you from finishing your investigation. A first aid kit is the only way to ensure that doesn't happen.

Flashlight: You never know what dark corners of the school you'll discover. A flashlight could help you find a clue that you otherwise would have missed.

Skeleton key: Locked door? No problem. Investigate any room in the old school with a skeleton key that opens every lock.

Pepper Spray: Defend yourself against criminals with a cannister of pepper spray. Simply spray this into an attacker's face—and then run for it.

Pocketknife: This handy little trinket is for cutting, prying, and countless other uses. You may need it to open a box—or who can guess what else?

Rope: You never know when you'll need a rope. It's ideal for climbing in and out of deep holes, setting traps, and tying up villains.

Voice Recorder: A recorded confession might be as good as a photograph of evidence. Keep your recorder close, in case you hear a "ghost."

**CHOOSE FIVE ITEMS,
THEN GO TO PAGE 20.**

You cannot pass on a chance to interview Randall. And since he's running with a limp, you'll have no trouble catching him. But you don't want to surprise him either.

"Hey, wait up!" you shout as you hurry after him.

Randall stumbles to a stop. He turns to look at you, his face an expression of total confusion. "Was that you in there?" he asks, sounding hostile.

"In the gym? No, I heard shouting, so I came to check it out."

Randall nods. "I didn't think so." He stares at you for a moment, studying you. "Do you go to school here? I don't think I've seen you before."

"No," you say.

"Then you shouldn't be in here," he says. "The school is haunted." Any hint of fear in his voice is gone.

"I've heard. So what are you doing here?" you ask.

His eyes drop, a sure sign that he's going to lie. "I, um, needed to get my homework."

You're about to ask Randall what he saw in the gym, but he looks up at you again. A wave of anger washes over his face. "Wait. What do you care why I'm here? This is my school, not yours. I've got things to do, and I want you gone. If I see you again, you'll be sorry."

He awkwardly storms away, hobbling on his injured foot. You can't help but wonder how he got hurt—and when. For that matter, he lied about why he was here. On top of that, he's up to something, and he wants you out of the school.

Was Randall really scared? Did he actually encounter a ghost in the gymnasium? Or was it all just part of his plot to shut down the school? You need to go inside that gym to see what else you can learn.

GO TO PAGE 35.

It's hard to imagine that a student could mastermind a scheme to shut down an entire school. That makes Mr. Jenkins a much more likely suspect. You decide to investigate him first.

You hurry down the long corridor, toward the school's large trophy case at the center of the building. The lights are off; the hallway's only source of illumination comes from the evening sun shining through the windows. It leaves the corridor dim enough to look like the setting for a horror movie.

As you pass farther down the throat of the school, the thick, stuffy air turns musty. Old Central probably has air-conditioning, but it feels like they don't use it. The fact that you aren't familiar with the school's layout adds to your anxiety. You're relying on the details that Irene gave you—and she never said a thing about the custodians' closet. Your best guess is that it's near the center of the building, right by the principal's office, the main entrance, and the school's large trophy case.

You pause next to the display, noticing that many of the sports and academic awards are already being packed into cardboard boxes. It means Irene was right: They've already decided to close Old Central. Tonight's vote is just a formality.

Just past the principal's office, you find a thick wooden door labeled "Custodians Only." You grab the doorknob and twist.

Eeeeeee!

A terrible noise chills you, despite the heavy air. From off in the distance comes the frantic sound of screaming.

Your instincts tell you to stay put, away from trouble. After all, screaming tends to attract adult attention—and the only adults in Old Central are the kind who would order you to leave. That would put an end to your investigation before it ever really began.

On the other hand, those screams might lead you to another clue. Or maybe someone's in trouble and needs your help.

WHAT WILL YOU CHOOSE TO DO?

Check out the screams.
GO TO PAGE 54.

Stay where you are.
GO TO PAGE 31.

"Well," she asks again, "are you mad?"

You shake your head. "Of course not. I'm worried the investigation may be too dangerous for you." You're not exactly lying. If she isn't the "ghost," then it is risky for her to be here. "And, yes, thank you for saving me yesterday," you add.

She relaxes her shoulders and smiles again. "I got you into this. I should share the risk. Besides, we'll be safer if we work together."

You nod. "You're probably right."

"So what's our next move?" asks Irene.

"We have five—er, I mean four suspects. We need to decide who to investigate first."

GO TO THE NEXT PAGE.

WHO WILL YOU INVESTIGATE?

Principal Haysen.

GO TO PAGE 15.

Mr. Jenkins.

GO TO PAGE 104.

Randall March.

GO TO PAGE 69.

Ms. Sanderson.

GO TO PAGE 111.

AFTER YOU'VE INVESTIGATED THEM ALL, GO TO PAGE 73.

You rummage through your backpack then pretend to be surprised. "It's not here!" you exclaim.

Principal Haysen sighs. "I tried so hard to avoid negativity today. Who do you think you're fooling?"

You try to protest, but she cuts you off. "It really doesn't matter. What matters is you are trespassing." She grabs your arm and squeezes. She doesn't let go until she's pulled you to her office and sat you in a chair.

"Shall I call your parents, or shall I call the police?"

The choice is obvious. You will be in (slightly) less trouble if your parents come and get you here versus coming to get you at the police station.

Everything that follows feels like a bad dream. There is a long and awkward wait, the principal adjusting her glasses and glaring at you. Then there are your parents, apologizing to Principal Haysen, raising their voices at you, and driving you home. There is your office in the garage getting taken apart, item by item. There is your "Kid Detective" sign being torn down for good.

You're out of business. Your mom and dad have shut you down. Your investigation into the Ghost of Old Central School is at an end.

GO TO THE NEXT PAGE.

THE END

Try Again

You make your way back to the center of the school and take the stairs to the second floor. The air up here is even more stifling. It presses in on you as if you're walking through a wet blanket. Your face flushes, and a drop of sweat slides down your back.

Irene doesn't seem to mind the heat. She walks faster and takes the lead down the hallway. She stops in front of the third door on the right. "It's this one: Ms. Sanchez's class," she says.

You swing open the door and step into the classroom. Sunlight filters in through the windows along the far wall, highlighting neat rows of desks. The teacher's desk has a flowering plant on it. Its bright pink blooms fill the air with a faint, sweet, earthy scent.

Irene stands next to a desk in the front row. "This is Randall's," she says.

Irene isn't in sixth grade. How does she *know where Randall sits*? It's just one more question for your sort-of employer to add to your list.

You lift the lid on Randall's desk and immediately frown. It's a messy pit. There's a green plastic ruler sitting in the front tray. You grab that and stir through the disaster, lifting wads of what could possibly be old homework assignments. You poke at a half-eaten sandwich, thankfully sealed in a plastic bag. The leftover food looks like it's doing its best to turn into another form of life.

"What's that?" asks Irene.

You jump. She's so quiet that you almost forgot she was there.

"Under the workbook," she adds.

Taking a closer look, you see a folded piece of light-blue paper sticking out from under a math workbook. You dig it out with the ruler and pinch the edge of it with two fingers.

It's crusty. A piece of what used to be cheese clings to the folded paper, and you peel it off with disgust. Your first stop after this will be a sink to wash your hands.

It's a note. The handwriting is surprisingly neat— better than yours.

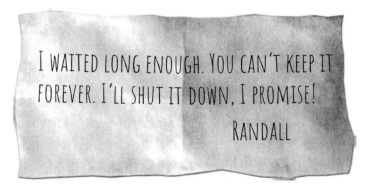

I WAITED LONG ENOUGH. YOU CAN'T KEEP IT FOREVER. I'LL SHUT IT DOWN, I PROMISE!

RANDALL

Irene reads it over your shoulder. "I'll shut it down?" she asks. "Is he talking about the school? That kind of makes him sound guilty."

"It's a good clue," you agree. "Let's take it with us."

You file it into your detective bag and are about to close the desk when you spot something taped to the underside of the lid: a piece of notebook paper. Written at the top are five words: "Locker ate tree ate." It looks like the same writing as the other note, so you assume it's Randall's. Under the word is a series of shapes.

$$\square + \square - \bigcirc$$

$$\triangle + \bigcirc + \square$$

$$\bigcirc + \triangle - \triangle$$

Irene pokes her head into the desk, studying the paper. "A locker ate a tree? What is he talking about?"

You shake your head. "No, think about it. What would you do if you couldn't remember your locker number or the combination? You'd write it down, but you wouldn't want anyone else to know what it says."

"Exactly," you say. "If we crack the code, we can get into Randall's locker."

"Ate tree ate. Ate tree ate . . . eight three eight!" exclaims Irene. "That must be his locker number. But what about the shapes? Any ideas?"

You think for a moment, staring at the shapes. They've got to be math problems with the addition and subtraction that's going on. The circle reminds you of a zero. Suddenly, it hits you. "How many sides does a circle have?" you ask Irene.

"None," she replies. "What are you talking about?"

You smile. "I think I cracked Randall's code."

WHAT IS THE CODE?

10-8-3.

GO TO PAGE 108.

8-7-0.

GO TO PAGE 92.

You've gathered a lot of information, but you don't feel much closer to solving this mystery. There is plenty to think about.

You see a set of double doors propped open, and you peek inside. The large classroom features a stage, of sorts, with risers. Long curtains hang on the back wall, from the ceiling to the floor. It must be the choir room.

You duck inside, cross through the front of the room, and take a left turn down a short hallway that's lined with smaller rooms: practice rooms. You swing open one of the doors. It makes a *whumpf* noise that tells you these rooms are soundproof.

Perfect. You settle onto the piano bench.

Irene remains standing, arms crossed. "What now?" she asks. "The board meeting is coming up fast."

You take out your notebook and page through it. "Let's start with Principal Haysen," you say. "We found Randall's phone in her office with the Halloween playlist. That could've been used to play over the P.A. system."

"But that doesn't mean she was the one who played them, right?" says Irene.

You nod. "Then there's the fact that she was looking for something in Ms. Sanderson's desk—possibly the book, but we don't know for sure," you add.

"What about Randall?" asks Irene. "What do we know about him?"

"Well, there are the notes," you say. "One threatens to shut everything down, and the other is from Mr. Jenkins, telling him to return all the ghost books in his locker. That doesn't look good."

"We also know Randall is still mad at the school for firing his dad—and because he might be getting kicked out soon," says Irene.

"Mr. Jenkins wanted Randall's books," you say. "He also had a stolen camera and a video of Ms. Sanderson going in and out of the basement. He didn't sound happy about this school, either."

"What do you suppose Ms. Sanderson was bringing in and out of the basement?" Irene asks.

"I'm not sure," you reply. "But she had that book about urban legends in her desk drawer. With the article about the old bank robberies and the possibility of the money being buried in the school basement, that gives her a motive for wanting the school closed; it would make her search a lot easier."

You pause for moment, deep in thought. Your stomach rumbles, and you realize it's time to go home for a quick lunch break.

"I'll meet you back here in an hour," you tell Irene, and then you make your way outside.

As you turn to head for home, you nearly bump into a petite woman with arms full of boxes. Her permed hair sticks to her forehead.

You recognize Ms. Sanderson. She's huffing from the effort of carrying so much, so you hold open the door for her.

"Thank you," she says. She pauses and gives you a hawkish look. "Are you a student here? I don't think I've seen you before."

"I'm new," you say. "Starting next week."

"If there is a next week," she answers.

"Right, the school might close," you say. "My parents were real upset about that since we just moved here."

"I bet," says Ms. Sanderson without a hint of emotion.

"Can I help you with those boxes?" you ask. It would be nice to see what's in them.

She instinctively pivots away from you, as if she's hiding something. She recovers quickly, though. "No thank you," she says. Then she hurries into the school, hauling her boxes with her.

* * *

At home, you park yourself in front of the computer with a peanut butter and jelly sandwich, enjoying the blissfully cool air that's blowing from the vent by your feet. Between bites, you try to dig up more information on "Cool" Judd Jones and the legend about him burying his loot in the school.

You don't find much that you didn't already know, but you do find an amount. You nearly choke on your sandwich when you read, "The estimated value of Jones' stash is well over $3 million."

You're about to finish up and head back over to the school when you decide to do one more quick search, something you should've done from the start. You type "Superintendent Gorter Old Central School" into the search bar and sort through the results.

The district's website should be a reliable source, so you click on the link. You find a page about the superintendent. It displays information about his role with the district, along with a picture of him with his whole family.

You freeze, staring at the picture.

Superintendent Gorter has no daughters.

GO TO THE NEXT PAGE.

THURSDAY
1:36 P.M.

You stand just inside the main school doors, waiting for Irene, your mind churning with questions. If Irene isn't Superintendent Gorter's daughter, then who is she? And why would she hire you to save the school?

You prop open the door with your foot to get a little air flowing, but it doesn't help. You feel like you're breathing through a lava tube.

You check your watch for the tenth time. Irene said she'd see you in an hour, but it's been nearly an hour and a half. As much as you want to confront Irene about her big lie, you still have a job to do—and not much time to do it.

Logically, there are two places to check out next: the basement and the gym. As hard as it is to admit, you're not too excited to go into either place alone.

It figures: The one time you actually want Irene to be around, she's a no-show. It looks like you're on your own. You let the door close and move into the gloom of the school. You must pick a spot to investigate.

GO TO THE NEXT PAGE.

WHERE WILL YOU INVESTIGATE?

The basement.

GO TO PAGE 105.

The gymnasium.

GO TO PAGE 100.

AFTER YOU'VE INVESTIGATED BOTH PLACES, GO TO PAGE 116.

"It's Principal Haysen!" you proclaim.

The room falls silent, and Principal Haysen looks at you with genuine confusion.

"That is a serious accusation," the Board President says. "Do you have proof?"

You thought you did. In fact, you were sure of it. But thinking back, the conclusion to which you jumped just doesn't make sense.

"I— I thought so," you mumble. Your cheeks blaze with embarrassment.

The rest of the evening's events pass like a bad dream. Your parents arrive, and there's apologizing to the entire school board, raising their voices at you, and driving you home. There's your office in the garage getting taken apart, item by item. There's your "Kid Detective" sign being torn down for good.

You're out of business. Your mom and dad have shut you down. Your investigating days are done.

GO TO PAGE 68.

"Quick," you whisper. "Hide."

Clutching the book and the article, you dive under the desk. Irene doesn't join you—which is good because there isn't room. You hope her hiding place is good.

You see an adult woman's legs stop right next to you. The drawer above your head is yanked open, and a small shower of dust settles on your head. Your nose begins to tickle, and you try to squeeze the itch away by flexing the muscles in your face. It doesn't work. The tickle grows worse and worse. You desperately try to will yourself not to sneeze. What comes out instead is a muffled *Grff!*

Principal Haysen bends down, and her surprised—then angry—face appears. She reaches under the desk, grabs your arm, and hauls you from your hiding spot. She is surprisingly strong.

"What are you doing here?" she demands.

You try to offer an explanation, but she cuts you off. "It doesn't matter. What matters is you are trespassing." She grabs your arm and squeezes. She doesn't let go until she's pulled you to her office and sat you in a chair.

"Shall I call your parents, or shall I call the police?"

The choice is obvious. You will be in (slightly) less trouble if your parents come and get you here versus coming to get you at the police station.

Everything that follows feels like a bad dream. There is a long and awkward wait, the principal adjusting her glasses and glaring at you. Then there are your parents, apologizing to Principal Haysen, raising their voices at you, and driving you home. There is your office in the garage, getting taken apart, item by item. There is your "Kid Detective" sign being torn down for good.

You're out of business. Your mom and dad have shut you down. Your investigation into the Ghost of Old Central School is at an end.

GO TO PAGE 68.

Without a light, it will be risky to proceed. But there's risk involved with solving any case, so you decide to forge ahead. This far underground, the tunnel can't be very long, and you need to know what's at the end of it to move your investigation forward.

Grit and pebbles press painfully into your palms as you crawl along. Your breath comes in short bursts; you've never liked enclosed spaces, and this is about as enclosed as it gets. It's as if you can feel the weight of the entire school squeezing in on you.

Inch by inch, you make your way down the tunnel. The overpowering smell of wet earth is your only companion.

You move your right hand forward and feel it snag on a wire. Instinctively, you press your wrist forward and *whump!* A tremor shakes the tunnel floor as specks of dirt rain down around you for a moment.

Then all is still. The darkness is absolute.

Panicking, you scooch backward as quickly as you can. Your feet run into something solid. You press into it. Then you kick at it, harder and harder. It doesn't give.

A small cry escapes your lips. Your mind races in a thousand directions and comes to one conclusion: You must have triggered a door when you hit that wire.

You fell into a trap.

Now you're alone. In the dark. All you can do is try to remain calm, breathe, and wait, but you can feel your panic rising. You hope that Irene will bring help before it's too late.

GO TO PAGE 68.

In a split second, you make your decision. You crawl toward the narrow opening in front of you, and you press yourself through it. At first, it seems as if you'll fit without much trouble, but the shifting sections catch up to each other with you half in and half out.

Your body feels like a crumpled piece of paper. All the air is squeezed out of you. You can't catch your breath—not to mention the pain in your stomach. A few more seconds of this, and you won't feel anything anymore.

Suddenly, your body goes numb. At least, that's what it feels like. But when you tumble forward, you realize that the gap must have widened again.

You pull your legs free at the last instant, just before the bleachers slam closed, becoming part of the gym wall again. You made it, but it was close.

You sit for a moment on the gym floor, arms around your knees, head bowed, and eyes shut. You silently thank yourself for not eating a bigger lunch.

When your heart slows back to normal and when you can take a breath without shaking, you stand up. Someone just tried to kill you again. This is getting personal. It's time to do some more investigating.

GO TO PAGE 79.

You dig into your backpack and pull out the skeleton key. You hold it up and say, "This should do the trick."

Irene tilts her head. "You have a key to the closet?"

"Something like that," you tell her. "This key works on a lot of doors." You slide the key into the keyhole and turn it. You smile to yourself when you hear that satisfying click of the bolt retracting.

You grab the doorknob and pull. The hinges squeal; they're in need of oil. The door swings wide, and you and Irene step into the dark.

"There's a light switch over here," says Irene.

You reach around her to flip the switch. A dim bulb springs to life above you, offering a dull and barely helpful glow over the contents of the closet.

Mops and brooms lean against the wall to your right, surrounded by various buckets on the floor. The shelves on the left are stuffed with cleaning supplies. So far, this is a bust. There's nothing here out of the ordinary.

Wait.

Against the back wall sits a stack of folded tarps. A cord pokes out from beneath it. What would a cord be doing in a stack of tarps?

You follow the cord to its source and pull out an old video camera—definitely not the latest technology.

Irene gasps. "What's that doing here? That belongs to the AV club. It was one of the things that went missing last week, one of the things stolen by the . . . well, by whoever's been stealing things."

"What else went missing last week?" you ask.

Irene thinks for a moment, tapping her chin. "Oh, I'm pretty sure the baseball coach mentioned a bag of baseballs. There were two computers from the computer lab, a bunch of library books, and four microscopes from the science room. And any posters or flyers that get hung up disappear, too."

You note these items in your notebook. Then you plug the camera into an outlet and turn it on. "Let's see what's on here," you say.

The tiny screen comes to life. At first, the picture is dark. Then there's a grunt, and the dark gives way to a hand, up close and personal, removing the lens cap. The picture is now a distant shot of a doorway.

"I know where that is," says Irene. "It's the stairway at the back of the school that goes to the basement. Why would someone video that?"

You soon get your answer.

The picture zooms in awkwardly then back out a bit. When it comes back into focus, you see a small woman with sharp features and permed hair hurrying toward the stairs, her arms carrying two large boxes.

She pauses, looks around as if making sure no one's watching, then disappears down the stairs.

"Ms. Sanderson," says Irene. "What's she doing?"

The video is so quiet for so long that you flinch when an angry voice mutters, "I told you so. Teachers sneaking around, hiding things. They're up to no good!"

After a few minutes, Ms. Sanderson appears without the boxes and hurries away from the doorway.

There's a cut in the recording, some fuzz, and then Ms. Sanderson again. This time, she's sneaking down the stairway without boxes and reappearing with a large bag slung over her shoulder.

"See what I mean?" asks the voice on the camera. "It's time to stop their messing about! This one—Sanderson—she's the worst of the lot!"

There are several more cuts in the video, punctuated by fuzz. Each time the picture comes back, you again see Ms. Sanderson sneaking into the basement and reappearing not long after. Sometimes she carries boxes down, sometimes up.

No matter what she carries, she always appears to check carefully to make sure no one sees her.

When there's no more footage to watch, you carefully stow the camera back where you found it. That's when you notice the list. Irene does too.

SPOOKY NOISES
MIST IN THE GYM
STUFF MISSING
GIRLS BATHROOM COLD SPOTS
SIXTH GRADE LIGHTS
GHOST IN AUDITORIUM

"Those are the weird happenings I was telling you about," she says. "Why would he write them down?"

"Either he's keeping track of the ghost, too, or that's his to-do list," you reply. "Let's get out of here." You flip off the lights on your way out, plunging the closet back into darkness.

As you step out into the hallway, your heart does a backflip: Mr. Jenkins is standing there, arms crossed, glaring at you and Irene.

"What are you doing?" he growls. His voice confirms that he was the person who made the recordings.

"Oh, um, we were just . . . looking for paper towels," you improvise. "Do you have any on hand?"

His eyes narrow, and you notice a *tattoo of a treasure map on his right forearm.*

"No? Oh, well, we'll try the bathroom," you say. "Thanks, anyway."

You feel Mr. Jenkins' eyes boring into your back as you and Irene walk quickly down the hall.

GO TO PAGE 66.

You grab the hammer, and you take a swing at the doorknob. The hammer bucks in your hand, and pain from the blow ripples all the way up to your shoulder.

You let out a growl of frustration and try again, hitting the doorknob even harder.

This time, the hammer spins from your grip, landing with a splash in the toxic liquid lapping at your tennis shoes. It's getting harder to breathe. Harder to think.

What were you doing just now? You were trying to hit something, but you can't seem to remember why.

You shake your head. Why is everything so fuzzy?

You slide to the floor, surprised by the sloshy splash that sounds like it's coming from a very long tunnel. That tunnel grows narrower and darker with each labored breath you take.

Your last coherent thought is a hope that someone finds you before it's too late.

GO TO PAGE 68.

Back in the hallway, you wipe the sweat from your eyes as you scan the locker numbers. It's cooler out here than in the classroom—but not by much. You find Randall's locker close to the stairway. It's blue and slightly dented.

Based on the contents of Randall's desk, you're not thrilled to look inside his locker. As you spin the numbers on the combination lock to line up at 8-7-0, some of the locker's possible contents flash through your mind: dirty gym socks, liquefied bananas in squishy brown skins, crumpled homework, mud-caked tennis shoes.

You swing the door wide to reveal . . . books.

A neat stack of books sits on the top shelf. Other than that, there's a navy blue sweatshirt hanging from the hook and a large pair of tennis shoes (not caked in mud) on the floor. All in all, the locker is surprisingly tidy.

Irene tilts her head slightly and reads the book titles. "*Famous Ghosts of the USA, Haunting at Gooseberry Hill, Spine-Chilling Tales*—these are all ghost stories."

You note the numbers on the spines. "It looks like they're from the school library," you add.

You heft the books off the shelf for a closer look. A piece of paper slides off the top of the stack, so you set the books back in the locker and grab the piece of paper.

> RANDALL—
>   Ms. SANDERSON SAID YOU
> HAVE THE BOOKS. PLEASE
>   RETURN THEM ASAP. I NEED
> TO SEE THEM RIGHT AWAY.
>   —MR. JENKINS

You add this note to your bag, as well. Then you close the locker—just in time. You hear footsteps on the stairs, so you signal to Irene. The two of you move quickly across the hallway, as if you were looking at a different locker.

HAVE YOU MET RANDALL?

Yes.

GO TO PAGE 135.

No.

GO TO PAGE 124.

You activate your device and shine a light down the tunnel, creating harsh shadows on the narrow, patchy walls. This far underground, the tunnel can't be very long, and you need to know what's at the end of it to move your investigation forward.

Grit and pebbles press painfully into your palms as you crawl along. Your breath comes in short bursts; you've never liked enclosed spaces, and this is about as enclosed as it gets. It's as if you can feel the weight of the entire school squeezing in on you.

Inch by inch, you make your way down the tunnel. The overpowering smell of wet earth is your only companion.

Your light catches a flash of something shiny. You stop and take a closer look. It's a mostly hidden wire that's been strung across the tunnel just a few inches above the floor. You can't be sure, but it appears to be a trigger of some sort—which would very likely spring a trap or signal an alarm.

You crawl carefully over the wire without disturbing it—not an easy task. As you move beyond the wire, your light splashes onto a pile of items: a bag of baseballs, mouse pads, posters, notebooks, pens and pencils, a bunch of cords, and a black box labeled "AV Club."

These are things that Irene said had disappeared—items taken by the "ghost." So the guilty person has definitely been down this extremely narrow tunnel and definitely set up that trap.

Scooting forward, you see the handle of a shovel. Beyond the shovel, the tunnel opens into an area that's big enough to stand in.

The floor is riddled with holes, mounds of dirt beside each one. The "ghost" is looking for the outlaw's treasure here—and now you know who the "ghost" really is.

You navigate your way back over the wire with almost no room to spare. You can't get out of this tunnel—and out of the basement—fast enough.

GO TO THE NEXT PAGE.

You leap up the basement stairs, two at a time, Irene trailing behind. The temperature increases with each jump. Leaving the chill of the basement, you start to sweat in earnest again.

"What's the fastest way to the board room?" you ask, wiping your brow. You hope you don't look too grungy after your tunnel adventure. You have to tell the school board members what you know, and there's no time to change. That meeting is coming up fast.

"I'm not sure," says Irene. "This way, I think."

She leads you down one hallway, then another. Before you know it, you wind up in front of the custodian's closet. At least you know where you are.

That's weird. The closet door is wide open.

You register the pounding footsteps behind you a moment too late. Hands on your back shove you roughly into the closet. You spin into a shelf, and several jugs smash to the floor, just as the closet door slams closed.

Pain lances through your shoulder—the shoulder on which the strap to your detective bag should be. You must have dropped it when you got shoved in here.

Panic threatens to overwhelm you, but you gather yourself and try to turn the door handle.

It's locked.

"Irene!" you call.

No answer.

Your eyes start to burn, and you notice puddles spreading around your feet. You nudge one of the smashed jugs so you can read the label.

The news isn't good.

You're standing in a growing pool of paint thinner, and the fumes are quickly filling this small, enclosed space. You know from working on house projects with your parents that paint thinner is highly flammable—and the fumes are toxic. If you don't get out of here fast, you'll get dizzy and tired and confused. Your brain will quit working and if no one finds you in time . . .

You decide not to finish that thought.

Maybe Irene has gone for help, but you can't count on it. Whoever shoved you into this closet—and you have a good idea who it was—may have taken Irene out of the picture, too.

Scanning the room, you spy a stack of rags. Quickly, you tie one over your nose and mouth as a makeshift mask. It may help to slow your intake of fumes.

You feel a fog starting to drift over your mind, and you shake your head to clear your thoughts.

Think, you tell yourself.

A harsh cough grips your burning throat. You blink hard and rub your eyes. You scan the shelves around you: cleaning spray, paint cans, mops, buckets, toilet bowl scrubbers, a bin full of tools, rubber gloves—wait! That's it!

You scramble through the bin full of tools, scattering them on the floor. You see two tools that might be useful. You can use a hammer to try and pound the handle off the door, which should also break the lock. Or you can use a screwdriver to try and pop the lock open.

Use the hammer.

GO TO PAGE 91.

Use the screwdriver.

GO TO PAGE 131.

"It's Irene Gorter!" you proclaim.

The room falls silent, until someone shouts, "Who?"

"She's a student here," you reply. "I'm not sure it's her real last name, though."

"That is a serious accusation," the Board President says. "Do you have proof?"

You thought you did. In fact, you were sure of it. But thinking back, the conclusion to which you jumped just doesn't make sense.

"I— I thought so," you mumble. Your cheeks blaze with embarrassment.

The rest of the evening's events pass like a bad dream. Your parents arrive, and there's apologizing to the entire school board, raising their voices at you, and driving you home. There's your office in the garage getting taken apart, item by item. There's your "Kid Detective" sign being torn down for good.

You're out of business. Your mom and dad have shut you down. Your investigating days are done.

GO TO PAGE 68.

You don't normally think of a gym as a scary place, but this is also the first time you've been in an empty gym, at a school that's supposedly haunted, in a place where someone recently tried to turn you into a Popsicle.

Plus, you've heard a few stories about haunted gyms, *like a place where students can hear a basketball being dribbled by the ghost of a former basketball player and another where a spirit randomly screams from time to time.*

This time, at least, the gym doesn't feel as empty as before. The bleachers had been folded closed and pressed up against the walls. Now they're open, filling some of the space on either side of the basketball court.

You see the door leading into the kitchen on the opposite wall, and you shiver despite the sticky air. You won't be going in there again. You rub your arms to get rid of the goose bumps that suddenly form.

Don't be silly, you chide yourself. *You're fine.*

Your eyes roam over the empty gym and land on a door that you didn't notice before. This one is along the wall directly to your right, tucked into the corner. The squeaks of your tennis shoes echo loudly as you step toward the door. Cringing, you try to walk more softly.

You pull the handle, and you're in luck: The door is unlocked. You flip on the light switch just inside the doorway and step into a huge equipment closet. There are stacks of flat seats with wheels—scooters for the little kids. There are giant bins full of dodge balls, soccer balls, and basketballs. Floor hockey sticks line the back wall, along with rolled-up nets for volleyball or badminton. There's even a shelf full of brightly colored and neatly folded parachutes. Oddly, one of the parachutes is stuffed to the side. In such an organized closet, that's worth a closer look. You lift a corner of the slippery fabric, and the whole parachute slides to the floor with a hiss, puddling around your feet.

You're left staring at a black box, a little bigger than a shoe box, with a rotating handle on top and a flat, circular nozzle on the front. It was hidden beneath the parachute, and if it's what you think it is, you've found the source of the creepy mist.

You pick it up and take a look at its side. The logo, "Fogger," confirms it. You've found a fog machine. You also notice a small remote control on the shelf. It's only a little bigger than an eraser, and it has a tiny antenna sticking out the top. Red buttons dot the front of it: "On," "Off," and "Set Timer." Whoever wanted to create a mysterious mist could have done it without even being in the gym.

You scoop the parachute from the floor and stuff it back on top of the fog machine. There's no sense in advertising the fact that you've been here.

Just as you flip off the light switch, you hear a noise in the gym: the bounce of a ball. Why did you have to remember that ghost story? You cautiously step outside the equipment closet and catch a glimpse of a basketball rolling behind the bleachers.

"Irene?" you say hesitantly.

There's no answer, but you think you hear footsteps. It must be her. She knew the places you wanted to check out after lunch. You duck into the shadows underneath the bleachers.

You don't see that basketball anywhere, so you step farther inside, dodging all the poles and levers that allow the bleachers to fold out and fold back in.

"Irene?" you repeat, louder this time.

You're nearly to the center, the bleachers towering above you, when your ears are filled with a loud and grinding mechanical noise. Groaning and scraping, the bleachers begin to press toward you. They're closing!

If you don't move fast, you'll be a squished version of the Ghost of Old Central School. You whirl around and look back the way you came. It's a straight path, but at the rate the bleachers are closing, you're not sure if you'll make it in time. On the other hand, different sections of the bleachers are closing at slightly different speeds. This has created a temporary gap between the sections. You're definitely close enough to make it, but is the gap big enough—and how long will the gap last? You don't want to get stuck.

Either way, if you make the wrong choice, things could get messy.

Hurry back.

GO TO PAGE 128.

Go through the gap.

GO TO PAGE 85.

Your shirt is already sticking to your back as you and Irene make your way toward the center of the school. Shadows play across the floors, and the silence seems to press against each step. You shiver despite the heat.

Just past the principal's office, you stop at the thick, wooden door labeled "Custodians Only." You grab the doorknob and twist. It feels like *déjà vu*; you tense in anticipation of the scream you heard last time you tried opening this door.

There's no scream, though, just the loud clang of the door's bolt catching against a strike plate.

Irene looks at you. "It's locked. Now what?"

DO YOU HAVE A SKELETON KEY?

Yes.

GO TO PAGE 86.

No.

GO TO PAGE 130.

The back stairwell must be the last place to get cleaned in the entire school. Your shoes grind on dirt and grit, making an unnerving *scritch-scratch* sound with each step you take.

The first set of stairs ends at a small landing and then continues down in the opposite direction. Then it opens into a grim, dingy hallway. At the end of that, a metal door is propped open with a box.

The one bonus of being down here is that it's cooler, even if it's damp and clammy. But it smells like old, wet gym socks.

You pause at the door, listening to the hisses and soft clanks that come from the maze of rusty pipes on the ceiling above you. There's just enough light down here to create misshapen shadows at every turn.

You move ahead cautiously, feeling as if you are walking into a horror story—like the ghostly tale of a famously haunted school basement in Ohio. *According to that legend, several children died in the basement, but their ghosts remained. The spirits of the children have been seen roaming the hallways of the school.*

You wish you hadn't thought of that, especially now.

A feathery hand brushes past your face, and you nearly scream. Then you exhale a short, nervous laugh as you wipe a sticky thread from your mouth. It's just a spiderweb. When your eyes adjust to the darkness, you see that the basement is full of them.

Short tanks and tall electrical cabinets sprout from the floor, some of them labeled and some with ancient, stained warning stickers that look half-chewed by rats. You notice a square cabinet with a well-worn "Air Conditioning (AC)" label on it.

You make the mistake of rushing toward it and *smack*! Stars explode in front of your eyes, and you reel backward. A dazed moment later, you realize that you hit a low-hanging pipe with your forehead. Wincing, you duck under the pipe and inspect the AC unit.

There's nothing unusual about it that you can see. Your toes kick something on the floor—something that is sticking out from under the cabinet.

You reach down and grab a mold-splotched manual, opened to a page labeled "operation." Mr. Jenkins is the one running this stuff down here. He's been doing it for years. Why would he need an instruction manual?

You see a gray, metallic box hanging from the wall, behind a giant metal tank that sports a nightmarish amount of hoses, pipes, and dials. It's the school's circuit breaker box. Its door is wide open.

Inside the box, there are three columns of black switches, each labeled with nonsensical codes, such as E47-52. Only a custodian would know what these mean.

Wait. One switch near the bottom of the second column has the words "6th grade" taped beneath it. Unlike the other labels you've seen down here, this one looks fairly new. It was obviously put here by someone who doesn't know what the codes mean. A few flips of this switch and everyone in the sixth grade experiences an "unexplainable" event: spooky, flickering lights.

This is a big clue. You mark it in your notebook and continue farther into the basement. You duck to avoid another low-hanging pipe and nearly trip over a box. You peel back the flaps to look inside.

Library books. In fact, the whole area back here is a jumble of boxes and bags. A quick check in a few of them confirms it: These are all books. Some of the boxes contain other things, too, like notebooks, pencils, posters, mouse pads—just junk. Could this be why Ms. Sanderson is sneaking into the basement? Was she even sneaking at all or just putting old books down here to get them out of the way? These are important questions.

GO TO PAGE 79.

Back in the hallway, you wipe the sweat from your eyes as you scan the locker numbers. It's cooler out here than in the classroom—but not by much. You find Randall's locker close to the stairway. It's blue and slightly dented.

Based on the contents of Randall's desk, you're not thrilled to look inside his locker. As you spin the numbers on the combination lock to line up at 10-8-3, some of the locker's possible contents flash through your mind: dirty gym socks, liquefied bananas in squishy brown skins, crumpled homework, mud-caked tennis shoes.

Time to find out what's really in there. You yank on the lock. Nothing happens.

Did you get the code wrong? Were the shapes even a code for Randall's locker? Now you're second-guessing yourself. Your face flushes, and although it doesn't seem possible, you start to sweat even more.

"Try again," says Irene. "We need to get in there."

You try the lock again—with no luck. You give it a third and fourth try with different numbers. You're concentrating so hard that you don't hear the footsteps until it's too late.

A look of surprise crosses Randall March's face as he rounds the top of the stairs and sees you and Irene at his locker. That surprise is quickly replaced by a scowl. "What are you doing?" he demands. He closes the distance fast for someone who's limping.

"Get away from my locker!" He grabs your shirt with a meaty fist and swings you around. He shoves you hard into the bank of lockers.

Your back takes most of the blow, but your elbow cracks against the metal in exactly the wrong spot, sending pain shooting through your arm. The crash echoes up and down the empty hallway.

You blink, and suddenly there's that meaty fist again, this time headed straight at you. You duck at the last instant. Randall howls as his would-be punch lands on a locker door instead.

Holding your injured arm, you make a dash for the stairwell—and you run directly into Mr. Jenkins.

He grabs your shoulder. "What's the hurry?"

Irene bolts, but Randall's not quick enough to get away. He ends up gripped by his shoulder on the other side of the angry custodian.

"Out!" yells Mr. Jenkins. He marches you down the stairs. "Think you hooligans can come in here and run around wrecking things? Who's got to clean up after you? Ever think about that?"

Mr. Jenkins shoves you and Randall out the front doors of the school. The sun hits you like a supercharged spotlight. You hear the lock slide closed, and you realize one thing for a fact: Your investigation is over.

GO TO PAGE 68.

Irene leads the way to the library on the school's second floor. It's not your typical school library. It looks more like two classrooms smashed together with a bunch of books thrown inside. There are rows of books to your far right, and a few study carrels are scattered throughout the room. Tall shelves are a jumbled mess to your left, as if the library is under construction.

You can't help but think of the tales you heard about the Peoria Public Library in Illinois. *As the story goes, the old library was built on cursed land. This reportedly proved to be true because the library's first three directors all suffered tragic fates between 1915 and 1924—a span of less than 10 years.*

One of the directors is said to haunt the library to this day. His spirit has been seen several times over the years, most notably in a basement doorway.

Ms. Sanderson, however, is no "ghost" . . . or is she?

As Irene described her, Ms. Sanderson is slender with sharp, crooked features. She has been the school's media specialist for eight years and has a reputation for being a little peculiar—and very superstitious. She's the type of person who never walks under ladders, avoids black cats, and throws salt over her shoulder for luck.

"Let's check out her desk," you suggest.

You open her top desk drawer and find yet another sign of the media specialist's odd nature: a book titled *Famous Myths & Urban Legends*. You pick up the book and quickly leaf through the pages.

A folded piece of paper slips from the book and falls onto the desk. You pick it up and recognize it as a newspaper clipping. The paper is yellow and faded; it feels like it might crumble in your hand. That means it's old—*really* old—like from when your grandparents were kids. You carefully unfold it.

"What's it say?" asks Irene.

You scan the content, making sure it's safe to share with a partner you don't trust. You decide it is, so you begin to read aloud:

"Even our fair town has felt the effects of the unscrupulous activity of famous bank robber 'Cool' Judd Jones. Evidence that Jones may have buried some of his unearned treasure in this very village has recently come to light. Though the exact location remains a mystery, authorities are diligently searching the city center and surrounding areas."

The article goes on to describe the bank-robbing career of "Cool" Judd Jones, listing all the banks he held up and how he was eventually caught.

"Interesting, but what does it have to do with Ms. Sanderson?" asks Irene.

"I don't know," you admit. You set down the article and return to the book. A third of the way through it, you come upon a highlighted passage.

"Listen to this," you say, and you read aloud again. "Little is known about the whereabouts of the stolen money. Jones himself hinted that he buried his loot in the basement of a school while he was on the lam. The exact location, however, is a secret that died with Jones."

Irene looks thoughtful.

"What is it?" you ask.

"Old Central School was named that for a reason," she says. "The school used to be in the center of town—like the city center mentioned in the article."

A detail clicks into place. You nod. "The treasure from this article—the stolen money—might be buried in this school's basement."

"I bet Ms. Sanderson thinks so, too," says Irene. "I also bet searching for that treasure would be a lot easier with the school closed."

"That gives her a motive," you say. "But it could also be a motive for any of our suspects—if it's true." You think of Irene. It could be a motive for her and her dad, too, although it wouldn't explain why she hired you in the first place.

You get a sinking feeling in your gut, one that means this investigation just got a lot more complicated.

As you glance again at Ms. Sanderson's desk, you notice her handwritten to-do list: "Finish londry, get grosheries, pack offise." *Ms. Sanderson is terrible at spelling.*

Your thoughts are interrupted by a shuffling noise in the hallway. The library's door starts to swing open. You need to find a place to hide—fast. You see two options close enough to work: You can squeeze between two bookshelves and hope this visitor doesn't look around too carefully, or you can hide under the desk and hope this person doesn't use the desk.

WHAT WILL YOU CHOOSE TO DO?

Hide by the shelves.

GO TO PAGE 127.

Hide under the desk.

GO TO PAGE 81.

"It's Randall March!" you proclaim.

The room falls silent, and Randall looks at you with genuine confusion.

"That is a serious accusation," the Board President says. "Do you have proof?"

You thought you did. In fact, you were sure of it. But thinking back, the conclusion to which you jumped just doesn't make sense.

"I— I thought so," you mumble. Your cheeks blaze with embarrassment.

The rest of the evening's events pass like a bad dream. Your parents arrive, and there's apologizing to the entire school board, raising their voices at you, and driving you home. There's your office in the garage getting taken apart, item by item. There's your "Kid Detective" sign being torn down for good.

You're out of business. Your mom and dad have shut you down. Your investigating days are done.

GO TO PAGE 68.

You've been able to answer most of the questions about the ghostly happenings around here—aside from who's behind it all. But there's still one place you haven't visited, and that's your next stop. You hope it presents some new leads because, after this, you're out of ideas.

Old Central's towering auditorium is glorious. It looks like something straight out of a history book. Row after row of cushioned, red seats stretch from wall to wall, with an aisle on either side of the center section. The walls themselves are decorated with white and gold trim. The stage is framed by massive red velvet curtains.

As you step inside the vast room, you're reminded of the adage: "Every theater is haunted."

"Yeah, right," you mutter.

You're a little suspicious that the lights are already on in here when they're off everywhere else in the building, but you wouldn't be able to see much if they weren't.

You walk to the edge of the stage, where the "ghost" was first seen. It reminds you of another ghost story you once heard. *There was a school in Michigan where all the student performers had a tradition of writing their names on a wall backstage. One of the students, a girl named Mary, tragically passed away before she could write her name. Yet somehow, a few days later, the word "Mary" mysteriously appeared on that wall. It was written upside down, at the top of the wall, 17 feet above the floor.*

You don't believe that story, but you catch yourself peering up at the backstage walls anyway.

"Hi, Blaze."

You jump and whirl around. There stands Irene.

She gives a small laugh. "Did I scare you?"

"No," you say irritably. "But you did lie to me."

"What do you mean?" she asks.

"Your dad? Whoever he is, he's not Superintendent Gorter. Is that even your last name?" you demand.

Her eyes widen, and she takes a step back. "Wha—How?" Her bottom lip begins to tremble.

"How did I find out? It wasn't rocket science. There's a family picture online, and you're not in it."

Irene stares at the floor. Her chin wobbles. She looks like the waterworks are going to start any minute—something you'd rather avoid.

"Why?" you ask.

"Why what?"

"Why did you hire me? If it's not for your dad, why don't you want your school to close? Why are we here?"

Her eyes begin to water. Yep, here it comes.

She sighs heavily.

This has to be about a boy.

"I have a boyfriend, Heath Winter," she admits.

Sometimes you hate being right.

"He's the star of our middle school baseball team— and he's my soulmate."

You roll your eyes.

Irene goes on. "If Old Central closes, the way it's been divided, we'll be at different schools. I won't get to see him anymore. It'll be the end of our relationship."

A flood of tears seems moments away, but to your relief, she regains her composure. "Are you mad?"

You don't answer. You remain quiet until the long, awkward silence becomes more than she can bear.

Finally, she whispers, "Will you still help me?"

You open your mouth to answer, but before you get the chance, a loud shriek rips through the auditorium. The lights switch off abruptly, plunging you and Irene into thick shadow. The curtains whisk closed with a mechanical whine.

You'd grab Irene's hand, but she's steadily backing up the aisle, away from the stage.

You notice a large bulge moving behind the curtain along the left side, heading for the center, as if whatever is there is looking for a way to get at you.

A large, decrepit hand emerges from between the curtains. You stand, frozen in place.

The shriek resolves into words. "Get out!"

You're not going to argue.

You turn on your heels and race up the aisle, toward the auditorium doors, just behind Irene. You hear pounding footsteps behind you, and a crazy thought flits through your mind. *Do ghosts make noise when they run? Do ghosts even run, or would they float?*

Whoever, whatever is behind you, it's closing in on you. It runs faster than you do.

You pick up the pace and sprint past Irene. You push the doors open and burst into the hallway. Sweat drips into your eyes, and your T-shirt clings to you like a soggy dishrag. As soon as Irene is clear of the doors, you slam them closed. You expect to hear a thump as the ghost plows into them, but that sound never comes. Whatever was chasing you seems to have vanished.

You and Irene don't wait around to be sure. You book it to the choir room and duck into the practice area. You collapse on the piano bench, panting and literally dripping sweat onto the floor.

Irene stands in the corner, arms crossed. She's not even out of breath, and it looks as if she's been sitting around, watching TV, rather than running pell-mell through a stiflingly hot and stuffy old school.

"Are you in track?" you ask between gasps.

"What?" asks Irene.

You shake your head. "Never mind."

The fact that she lied to you still irritates you, but you may as well see this case to the end. You're almost there. You're one clue away from solving this mystery, and you know where to look.

"I know where to go," you say.

Irene's face lights up. "You're still on the case?" she asks hopefully. "Even after I lied to you?"

"I don't trust you," you admit. "But I'm not done."

Irene looks like she's going to hug you but thankfully holds back. After that awkward moment, she asks, "So where are we going now?"

Unfortunately, it's the last place in this school you want to go. "Back to the basement."

GO TO THE NEXT PAGE.

THURSDAY
6:02 P.M.

"Are you sure we need to go down there?" asks Irene. She sounds as nervous as you feel.

"I'm sure," you reply.

You lead her down the stairwell, past the propped-open metal door, and into the heart of the basement. You duck to avoid another low-hanging pipe.

Moving on, you keep your head low; you've learned your lesson. And it's a good thing, too. Otherwise, you wouldn't have noticed the hole yawning from the floor. It's deep enough that whoever dug it had to prop a ladder inside to climb in and out.

Could this be where "Cool" Judd Jones buried his loot? There's only one way to find out.

"Stay here," you tell Irene. You take a deep breath and then climb down the ladder.

When your feet hit the bottom, you turn around. There's barely any light filtering down from above, but it's enough to see a dark area at about knee level. You squat and peer into the narrow tunnel. The hole is barely big enough for you to crawl into, and it's completely black inside. You need something to shine in there, like a flashlight or a mobile phone.

DO YOU HAVE EITHER ONE?

Yes.

GO TO PAGE 94.

No.

GO TO PAGE 83.

Do you need some help solving this mystery? No problem! Even the greatest detectives don't do it alone. After all, Sherlock Holmes has Dr. Watson and Batman has Robin. Let's take a look at what we know about this mysterious individual.

First, the villain is someone who doesn't know how the basement controls work. This person can't be anyone who was with you when you saw the "ghost" in the auditorium, and it is someone who can run fast—without any injuries. Finally, the criminal has to be kind of small or skinny to fit into the basement tunnel.

With all of that evidence, there is only one person it could be.

GO TO PAGE 134.

A student's eyes widen in surprise as he rounds the top of the stairs and sees the two of you. You recognize him from an Internet search you did at home: It's Randall March. He's *tall for his age with an athletic build*. His expression is quickly replaced by a scowl.

He must have *twisted his ankle or hurt his foot. He's walking with a limp*. He stumbles to his locker, staring at you the whole way, studying you. "Do you go to school here?" he asks. "I don't think I've seen you before."

"No," you say.

"Then you shouldn't be in here," he tells you. "The school is haunted."

"I've heard. So what are you doing here?" you ask.

His eyes drop, a sure sign that he's going to lie. "I, um, needed to get my homework." He looks up again. "What are you doing here?" he demands.

You motion to your bag. "Just taking some photos before the school closes for good," you say.

"Yeah? Why do you care?" asks Randall.

"It's a project for my social studies class," you say smoothly. "It's too bad about your school. Do you know where you'll go once it's closed?"

Randall runs a hand through his dark hair. He barks out a frustrated laugh. "Does it matter?"

"What do you mean?"

"I mean, I won't even go here, anyway, even if the old dump stays open. They're kicking me out. Haysen says I have too many *incidents*." Randall takes a step toward you, fists clenched. "Can you believe that?"

Maybe, you think.

Irene remains silent, worriedly watching you both.

"That's not why I'm getting expelled," says Randall. "You want to know what they did? They canned my dad for nothing—and now they're after me." He stops alarmingly close to you, towering over you. He pokes your forehead. "Put that in your report."

Your heart is pounding more loudly than a bass drum, but you refuse to be intimidated. "Your dad worked here?" you ask. "Was he fire— um, let go?"

Randall considers you for a moment. Then he shrugs and takes a step back, all the anger draining from him. "He was the custodian before *Mr. Jenkins*—about *four years* ago. And my dad didn't do anything wrong. He noticed things is all. Went to that dumb board with a list of stuff. He was way better than Jenkins is."

"He did a better job?" you ask.

"Yes, he did a better job!" snaps Randall. "You think my dad would go *digging through the trash* like

Jenkins? Always *hanging around the library*—and stuff goes missing when he's been in a room."

Remembering Randall's desk and the new-life-form sandwich, you're a bit surprised that Randall is so fussy about the cleaning.

"Wow, that's interesting. Well, thanks for the chat," you say, sliding from your spot between Randall and the locker bank. "But I have to keep working on my report."

"Whatever," replies Randall. He spins away from you and trudges toward his classroom.

You wonder why he's here, but your opportunity for asking questions has passed.

As you make your way down the stairs, you turn to Irene. "You were awfully quiet. You could have chimed in, you know," you say with a hint of irritation.

"You had it under control," she says.

You snort. "Like when he backed me up against the lockers and poked his finger at my head?"

"Yes, like that."

You blow out a frustrated sigh. At least you found out some good information.

GO TO PAGE 66.

"Quick," you whisper. "Hide."

Clutching the book and the article, you lunge toward the jumbled bookshelves, slip between them, and hunch low to the floor. Irene silently slides in beside you. It's a good thing she's so *slim*.

From your position, you have a narrow view of Ms. Sanderson's desk, just enough to see Principal Haysen step over to it and slide open the drawer where you found the book and the newspaper clipping. She digs in the drawer and grows increasingly agitated.

She lets out a growl of frustration. "Where is it?" she mutters. "It was here. I know it was."

She slams the drawer closed, pulls open the other drawers, and slams those shut, too. She runs her fingers through her hair, staring at the desk. You can't help but notice that her weirdness has really toned down. Is it all just an act? Before you can think any more about that, she storms angrily from the library.

You breathe a shaky sigh of relief. You look at the book in your hands. Is it Principal Haysen's? Did Ms. Sanderson take it? Is the principal looking for Jones' loot or is Ms. Sanderson? You have more investigating to do.

GO TO PAGE 66.

There's no chance you'll fit through the bleachers, and you don't like tight spaces anyway. You'll take your chances going back the way you came.

You spin and hurry toward the rapidly narrowing opening at the edge of the bleachers. All you can hear is the grinding noise of the seats sliding closed—that and your own panicked heartbeat.

You're almost there. You're going to make it with time to spare.

Until your foot gets snagged on a lever.

You trip and slam onto the gym floor. Stars explode in front of your eyes. All the breath leaves your body.

The pain doesn't register, at first, but it will. The bleachers are almost closed, and your time is up. You're about to become a permanent addition to the history of Old Central School.

GO TO PAGE 68.

"It's Mr. Jenkins!" you proclaim.

The room falls silent, and Mr. Jenkins looks at you with genuine confusion.

"That is a serious accusation," the Board President says. "Do you have proof?"

You thought you did. In fact, you were sure of it. But thinking back, the conclusion to which you jumped just doesn't make sense.

"I— I thought so," you mumble. Your cheeks blaze with embarrassment.

The rest of the evening's events pass like a bad dream. Your parents arrive, and there's apologizing to the entire school board, raising their voices at you, and driving you home. There's your office in the garage getting taken apart, item by item. There's your "Kid Detective" sign being torn down for good.

You're out of business. Your mom and dad have shut you down. Your investigating days are done.

GO TO PAGE 68.

You shrug. "Maybe the key is hidden around here." You scan the immediate area, looking for a secret place where a key might be kept.

Finding none, you come up with a new idea. "I can try picking the lock."

"Have you done that before?" asks Irene.

"No, but I've seen it done in movies." You wish you were joking.

You aren't sure where to begin, so you bend down and stare into the lock, trying to figure out what you might use in place of a key. You're concentrating so hard that you don't hear the footsteps until it's too late.

A look of surprise crosses Mr. Jenkins' face as he sees you at his closet door. That surprise is quickly replaced by a scowl. "What are you doing?" he demands.

Irene bolts, but Mr. Jenkins grabs your shoulder. "Out!" he yells. He marches you toward the exit. "Think you can come in here and run around wrecking things? Who's got to clean up after you? Ever think about that?"

Mr. Jenkins shoves you out the front doors of the school. You hear the lock slide closed, and you realize one thing for a fact: Your investigation is over.

GO TO PAGE 68.

You grab a thin, flathead screwdriver and jam it into the lock.

Nothing happens.

You let out a growl of frustration and try again, this time twisting the screwdriver with as much force as you can muster. The lock pops. You spill out the open door and into the hallway.

You rip the rag from your face and devour gulps of fresh air.

You might still make it to that meeting. Grabbing your bag, you take off at a sprint.

You follow the buzzing noise of a frustrated crowd and burst into the school's conference room at 6:59 p.m., leaving a trail of dirt and toxic fumes. Luckily, only a few people notice your bizarre entrance.

You hope Irene is safe, but you don't see her anywhere in the room.

Eight people, including Superintendent Gorter, sit on three sides of an enormous conference table, talking grimly. The chairs for others to observe the meeting are filled with staff members, teachers, parents, community members, and students. People who weren't early enough to get a seat line what little wall space is left. The room is energized with nervous anticipation.

You clutch your bag and watch the clock turn from 6:59 to 7:00. This is it.

As the meeting begins, the Board President speaks to the crowd. "We have a duty tonight to vote on the future of this school," she says.

There's a surge of grumbling from the crowd.

She holds up her hands to quiet them. "Before we vote, we will open the floor for final comments. This is not a light decision—"

"Your decision's already been made!" shouts Mr. Jenkins from the back corner.

You hadn't even seen him there. Now that you scan the crowd, you also see Ms. Haysen, Ms. Sanderson, and even Randall March, who is sitting next to a man that's unmistakably his dad.

"There will be order, or you will be removed," says the Board President smoothly. "As I was saying, we will now open the floor for comments." She looks over her glasses at the crowd. "Brief comments."

Your hand shoots into the air before anyone else can even think about it.

"Come on up," says the Board President. "State your name and connection to the school. Then *briefly*," she emphasizes again, "give your comments."

You approach the conference table and address the board. "My name is Blaze Bailey. My connection to the school is . . . complicated," you say. "But that's not important. Old Central School isn't haunted. Someone has been sabotaging the school in an intentional effort to shut it down."

The crowd erupts with frenzied sound, and it's several minutes before the Board President regains control.

"That's quite an accusation, especially for a student," says the Board President. "Do you have any proof?"

"Yes, I do," you say. "In fact, I know who the Ghost of Old Central School really is."

GO TO THE NEXT PAGE.

WHO DID IT?

Irene Gorter.

GO TO PAGE 99.

Ms. Haysen.

GO TO PAGE 80.

Mr. Jenkins.

GO TO PAGE 129.

Randall March.

GO TO PAGE 115.

Ms. Sanderson.

GO TO PAGE 138.

DO YOU NEED HELP? GO TO PAGE 123.

Randall March's eyes widen in surprise as he rounds the top of the stairs and sees the two of you. That expression is quickly replaced by a scowl. He limps the rest of the way to his locker.

"What are you doing here?" he demands.

You motion to your bag. "Just taking some photos before the school closes for good," you say.

"Yeah? Why do you care?" asks Randall. "You don't even go here."

"It's a project for my social studies class," you say smoothly. "It's too bad about your school. Do you know where you'll go once it's gone?"

Randall runs a hand through his dark hair. He barks out a frustrated laugh. "Does it matter?"

"What do you mean?"

"I mean, I won't even go here, anyway, even if the old dump stays open. They're kicking me out. Haysen says I have too many *incidents*." Randall takes a step toward you, fists clenched. "Can you believe that?"

Maybe, you think.

Irene remains silent, worriedly watching you both.

"That's not why I'm getting expelled," says Randall. "You want to know what they did? They canned my dad for nothing—and now they're after me." He stops alarmingly close to you, towering over you. He pokes your forehead. "Put that in your report."

Your heart is pounding more loudly than a bass drum, but you refuse to be intimidated by this bully. "Your dad worked here?" you ask. "Was he fire— um, let go?"

Randall considers you for a moment. Then he shrugs and takes a step back, all the anger draining from him. "He was the custodian before *Mr. Jenkins*—about *four years* ago. And my dad didn't do anything wrong. He noticed things is all. Went to that dumb board with a list of stuff. He was way better than Jenkins is."

"He did a better job?" you ask.

"Yes, he did a better job!" snaps Randall. "You think my dad would go *digging through the trash* like Jenkins? Always *hanging around the library*—and stuff goes missing when he's been in a room."

Remembering Randall's desk and the new-life-form sandwich, you're a bit surprised that Randall is so fussy about the cleaning.

"Wow, that's interesting. Well, thanks for the chat," you say, sliding from your spot between Randall and the locker bank. "But I have to keep working on my report."

"Whatever," replies Randall.

He spins away and trudges toward his classroom. You wonder why he's here, but your opportunity for asking questions has passed.

As you make your way down the stairs, you turn to Irene. "You were awfully quiet. You could have chimed in, you know," you say with a hint of irritation.

"You had it under control," she says.

You snort. "Like when he backed me up against the lockers and poked his finger at my head?"

"Yes, like that."

You blow out a frustrated sigh. At least you found out some good information.

GO TO PAGE 66.

You notice Ms. Sanderson. She's screened by the sheer number of people in the room, but she's sliding along the wall toward the door.

"Ms. Sanderson," you call.

She freezes for a moment and then bolts for the exit. Instinctively, the crowd blocks her way.

She turns slowly and levels you with a venomous gaze. "That is a serious accusation. Do you have proof?"

You lay out how the "ghost" caused the flickering lights with the labeled circuit breaker box and how the fog machine in the gym closet could've easily been used to create a spooky mist. Simple manipulation of the air-conditioning vents covers the unnaturally cold spots in the bathroom, and the instruction manual by the AC unit in the basement is a dead giveaway that someone was reading up on its operation. You also detail the "vanished" items you found in the basement. "I think you'll find her fingerprints on all of it," you conclude. "Plus, there's a trail of additional evidence, too."

"Why would anyone do all of that?" asks a random voice from the audience.

"To find the multi-million-dollar treasure," you say.

Again, the Board President has to calm the ruckus caused by your words.

Ms. Sanderson, trapped by several people at the back of the room, calls out, "I would have found it, too!"

"No, Mr. Jenkins was on to you," you say. "He even has video evidence."

He gives you a nod, and you continue. "You needed this school closed before he—or anyone else—stopped you—or got to the treasure first."

"Ladies and gentlemen," says the Board President, "we are going to take a recess to consider what we've learned. We will reconvene tomorrow evening at 7 p.m." She turns and speaks directly to you. "And you will be here, too."

GO TO THE NEXT PAGE.

EPILOGUE

You leave Ms. Sanderson in the capable hands of the school board. You slip out of the unbearably noisy room and into the peace and quiet of the hallway. Your footsteps echo as you walk toward the main entrance. One of the doors is propped open, and you hear rain hitting the pavement outside. A blissfully cool draft of air swirls in; the heat wave has finally broken.

You spot Irene standing by the trophy case. Thank goodness she's safe. She smiles and waves. You wave, too. She motions for you to follow her and then takes off. She turns a corner, and you get there just in time to see her round another corner.

A few more twists and turns, and you arrive at the girls' bathroom—the same one you escaped into after your near-disaster in the deep freeze. You hesitate for a moment. Did she go in there? What if she simply needs to use the restroom? That would be awkward.

No, she wanted you to follow. Your detective sense tells you to keep going.

"Irene?" you call.

The air in the bathroom is frigid. You rub your arms to smooth the sudden goose bumps.

A *thump* comes from the last stall.

You move farther into the room. "Irene?" you call again. There's still no answer.

This is getting weird. Where is she?

You knock on the door to the last stall. Then, tentatively, you push it open. There's a broken lock hanging from the door, and it takes only a moment to realize that, technically, it's not even a stall. There's no toilet, and the side wall is a hodge-podge of wooden boards. Lower down, near the floor, you spot something different. Etched into the old wood in all capital letters are three words: CITY CENTER WELL.

An idea forms in your mind, and it only takes a few minutes to tear down the rickety wooden boards. Behind them, you find a round, stone well. You peer down into the blackness—and catch a damp, musty smell right in the face. You spot a hand crank. It looks like there's still a rope attached.

Why not? you decide. You start to turn the crank.

After a few grudging, creaky turns, the handle spins faster. You hear something clanking on the sides of the well as it swings back and forth on its journey upward.

You hope it's nothing gross, and you're in luck. It's just a rusty bucket. You let out the breath that you didn't realize you were holding.

Surprisingly, the bucket is dry. Rather than water, it contains an old, stained burlap sack.

Your heart pounds as you take a peek inside. You see a little gold, a little cash, and a rolled-up piece of paper.

You carefully unroll it and find a map: specifically, a map that leads to the hiding place where "Cool" Judd Jones stashed his loot so many years ago. Ms. Sanderson was looking in the wrong place all along.

With shaking hands, you roll the map back up, grab the sack, and make a quick exit. You'll have a lot to show them at tomorrow night's follow-up meeting.

Irene should really go, too. You wonder again where she is right now.

Maybe you made a mistake. Maybe she went into a different room.

On a hunch, you return to the trophy case again. You scan the team photos. You remember Irene's "soulmate," Heath Winter, and you take a closer look at the baseball team's photo. There are three rows of players, and you quickly read through their names.

Then you read through their names again. There is no Heath Winter. Irene lied again.

* * *

Back at home, you do an Internet search for "Irene Gorter," not really expecting to find anything. After all, it's doubtful that Gorter is even her last name.

Three links down you find a book reference: *Mysteries and Puzzling Cases: 1993 Edition.*

The highlighted passage details a 1993 case of a student who went missing. Her name was Irene Gorter, and she was last seen entering the girls' bathroom at Old Central School. She was never seen again.

GO TO THE NEXT PAGE.

CONGRATULATIONS!

You solved
The Ghost of
Old Central School!

Choose your next adventure.

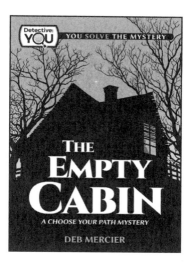

Available wherever books are sold

THE SCIENCE OF DEDUCTION

As discussed on page 6, we use deductive reasoning every day, whether we know it or not. It is basically using known facts to fill in the blanks or to come up with a logical solution. For example, let's pretend your Uncle Eddie is allergic to kiwi fruit. You have two choices of juice to serve him. One juice contains 10% kiwi fruit juice, and the other contains no kiwi fruit juice. Which juice would you serve him? The juice without the kiwi fruit in it, of course! (You like Uncle Eddie.)

That's deductive reasoning: using known information to make a logical deduction, or conclusion.

Of course, most of the deductions you make don't take very long. Truly, you don't even think about the ones you make countless times every day. But if you know what deductive reasoning is, it can help you figure out bigger, more complex issues.

Deductive Reasoning, Math Style

Mathematicians, teachers, and students use deductive reasoning when they solve certain math problems. Take a look at this:

X is the same as A. Y is the same as A. Therefore, we can deduce that X is the same as Y.

Here's another way of looking at it:

$$X = A$$
$$Y = A$$
$$\longrightarrow X = Y$$

Let's take it a step further. X equals 5. Y equals 5. So we can again deduce that the values of X and Y are equal. Here's another way of looking at it:

$$X = 5$$
$$Y = 5$$
$$\longrightarrow X = Y \text{ (because } 5 = 5\text{)}$$

Check it out: You just deduced your way through an algebra problem!

Deductive reasoning also comes in handy when you are faced with a word problem. Think of it like solving a mini-mystery. Try this one:

Mom is driving you to soccer practice. You leave at 10:15 a.m. You get to the field at 11 a.m. How long did it take your mom to drive you to practice? You can deduce that it took Mom 45 minutes to get you there. Either soccer practice is far away, or Mom drives slowly!

Deductive Reasoning, Science Style

Scientists also use deductive reasoning quite often. Let's pretend a new species of animal was discovered just last week in your neighborhood. A team of scientists is studying this critter in its natural habitat.

So far, they have observed a few traits, and they are keeping a list:

- It has purple fur.
- It eats acorns and potato chips.
- It has a pouch.
- When startled, it jumps like a basketball player.

Just from these observations, scientists can begin to draw a few conclusions. Here's an example:

Almost all marsupials have a pouch. This animal has a pouch. Therefore, this animal might be a marsupial.

Logical, right?

That brings us to another point, though: Deductive reasoning can backfire if it's not used correctly. Given the information gathered above, here's an example of deductive reasoning gone wrong:

Basketball players jump high. When startled, this animal jumps like a basketball player. Therefore, this animal might be a basketball player.

No, that's jumping to the wrong conclusion!

Here's the problem: When it comes to deductive reasoning, a person can "overgeneralize." That means we can make mistakes if we don't carefully consider each statement before making a conclusion.

Here's another rotten example: Bananas are yellow. My sister's shirt is yellow. Therefore, my sister's shirt is a banana.

No, that's a fruitless deduction! It may be true that bananas and my sister's shirt are yellow. However, this deduction is forgetting a very important fact: There are tons of yellow things in this world that aren't bananas.

We can turn this into a logical deduction this way: Bananas are yellow. My sister's shirt is yellow. Therefore, my sister's shirt is similar in color to a banana.

Now that you're a master in the art of deduction, go out there and deduce. For example, you might notice that there are no more words on this page and deduce that it's time to turn to the next one!

SOLVE ANOTHER CASE

Do you want more mystery? Check out
The Empty Cabin *by Deb Mercier,*
another book in the Detective: You series.

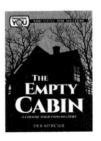

Something's wrong. Loretta's never late. In fact, she insists that if you're on time, you're late; and if you're early, you're on time. You check your watch again: 7:33.

You walk around to the front of Cabin #4 with an uneasy feeling in the pit of your stomach. The windows reflect the soft morning light like blank, unseeing eyes. Maybe Loretta forgot. It's an adult thing. Your parents can't remember where their keys are half the time.

But Loretta never forgets.

You step onto the tiny deck and approach the front door. You raise your hand and give the screen door a few quick raps. The door shuts with a thump; it must have been open just a bit when you knocked. You listen but hear nothing other than the wind in the trees.

You open the screen door and try the cabin door. It's unlocked. That's normal; only the city people lock their cabin doors up here. You ease the door forward and poke your head inside. The cabin is thick with shadows.

You slip inside and call Loretta's name. It's so still and quiet that you hear the clock above the sink ticking.

The Murphy bed is pulled down and the blankets are rumpled. A quick look in the tiny bathroom confirms it: Loretta's not here.

You turn back toward the door. Something under the kitchen table catches your eye.

You stoop down and pick it up, taking in a sharp breath. It's a rag soaked with blood. You drop it and fumble your way outside.

A few gulps of cool morning air clear your head. As you hurry off the deck and around the side of Cabin #4, you spy a flash of light up the hill to your left. There is a man on Cabin #2's deck, looking at you through binoculars.

Why is Edward spying on you—or was he hoping to see Loretta? You shake your head. You can't think about that right now; you have a decision to make. Should you go straight to your parents and tell them about Loretta's disappearance and the blood-soaked rag? If she's hurt, you have to move quickly. But maybe there's a note by the trailhead. Is it worth taking the time to check?

What will you choose to do?

ABOUT THE AUTHORS

Deb Mercier lives in greater Minnesota with her husband, dogs, and outdoor critter friends. She writes books for young readers and works as a technical writer at Douglas Machine, Inc. When Deb's not writing, you can find her wandering the trails on bike and on foot, saving turtles from roadways, and playing flute in the Central Lakes Symphony Orchestra.

Ryan Jacobson is an award-winning author. He has written more than 60 titles—from comic books to Choose Your Path adventures. Ryan prides himself on creating high-interest books for children and adults alike, so he can talk picture books in kindergarten, ghost stories in high school, and other fun stuff in between. He lives in rural Minnesota with his wife and two sons.